I0545690

Bugging Nate

by

JoMarie DeGioia

PUBLISHED BY:

Bailey Park Publishing

Copyright © JoMarie DeGioia 2018

All rights reserved. No part of this book may be reproduced or transmitted in any form or by any electronic or mechanical means, including photocopying, recording, or by any information storage and retrieval system, without the written permission of the publisher, except where permitted by law.

ISBN: 978-1-944181-20-8

Bugging Nate

Book Eleven of the
Cypress Corners Series

by

JoMarie DeGioia

Chapter 1

Cypress Corners, Florida

Becky Rollins got ready for work on Monday morning, humming to herself. Today was a big day for her, this windy Monday in March. A marking of an anniversary she'd never imagined when she'd snagged this job five years ago today. She slipped on her light green polo shirt emblazoned with the Cypress Institute logo, and then finished her casual uniform with a pair of khaki shorts and white Keds.

After pulling her long hair up into its usual high ponytail, she swept on some lip gloss and was good to go. She might not have a glamorous job, and the slick corporate clothes and shoes that went with it, but she was gainfully employed at a place she loved. That had to count for something. She'd worked hard to prove herself, and her life finally felt like it was her own.

She stepped out of her condo and headed down the stairs to the one-car garage set at the back of her unit. Her place was situated not too far from the center of Cypress Corners, so most days she left the used Prius she'd bought from her friend Claire Chapman and hopped onto her cruiser bicycle. Sure, the bike made her feel about seventeen years old. It was keeping with the spirit of Cypress, however.

Cypress Corners, her home for over a decade now, sat on over ten thousand acres of some of the prettiest land in Central Florida. With about seventy percent of it set aside for conservation of native plants and animals, it was unusual in the best way. It had once been wild grazing and ranch land, and the Cypress Institute oversaw the town to ensure that those native plants and animals weren't encroached upon by overdevelopment.

The town had been developed over fifteen years ago, but it appeared much older and more established than that. It featured upscale retail, state-of-the-art homes and an award-winning golf course. Then there was the small-town square. Picturesque and homey, it offered residents and visitors just about everything they might need.

Becky knew that most of the folks in the nearby city of St. Cloud referred to Cypress as Stepford. It did look pretty darn perfect, and the town square with its brick-front shops and old-fashioned street lamps looked like something out of a movie.

She had moved here with her family just in time to start high school in the brand new one just across the way. Her

family was still here, too. All but her father, who had passed
away not long after the move. Not only was that a shock,
since the massive heart attack seemed to come out of
nowhere, it was also heartbreaking, because he had loved the
entire concept of Cypress before they'd even looked at the
first available property. On bright mornings like this, she
missed him the most.

She was far from alone, though. Her mother ran the
Cypress Inn, where her younger brother still lived. She'd
bought her condo just before Thanksgiving of last year and
her older sister, Joy, had recently moved out to shack up with
her hunky cowboy boyfriend on the far lakeshore.

Wheeling her bike out of the garage, Becky pushed the
button on her key fob to shut the door. She clicked her tongue
and pulled out the ponytail holder before pushing her helmet
onto her head.

"Every day," she murmured, slipping the holder over
her wrist.

The sun was peeping through the tall sycamores lining
the main road as she rode her bike the mile and a half to the
town square. It was spring in Cypress Corners, which in
Central Florida meant that flowers were blooming and grass

was bright green. It also meant that her allergy medicine was working overtime. There were a few cars on the road, mostly driven by those unfortunate folks who worked outside of Cypress, on their way to Melbourne to the east or Orlando to the northwest. Becky was pleased to her toes that she lived and worked right here.

The Cypress Corners Institute sat across the street from the Sales Center on the square, and its proximity was no accident. Mr. Forbes, the developer, worked closely with Dr. Robbins. The doc was the director and the heart of the Institute, and she couldn't ask for a nicer boss. Genial and possessing an absentminded professor vibe, he instilled dedication in everyone who worked for him. She certainly counted herself among his fans, and had from the time she used to volunteer there. Hadn't he hired her on full time before her last year of undergrad at the University of Central Florida was complete?

She circled around back and parked her bike in the rack. She locked it tight and took off her helmet.

"Ugh, helmet hair," she grumbled.

Finger-combing through her thick waves, Rollins-red like her mother's and brother's, she pulled it up into a ponytail for the second time that day. Tucking her helmet under her arm, she headed inside and made her way to the reception area.

The sunlit space reflected the Institute's worthy agenda, in her opinion. Decorated in the colors of true Florida—rich greens, soft tans, and clear blues—it was filled with handmade rattan furniture and breathtaking photos of native flora and fauna hanging on the textured walls. Her desk, the command center as Dr. Robbins teased her, was as neat as she'd left it Friday afternoon. There was a noticeable difference today, however. A very large, very colorful potted plant sat smack in the middle of her desk.

"Harmony," Becky said with a smile.

Her friend and idol, Harmony Brooks Chapman, was the plant conservationist at the Institute, and put the needs of the flora first and foremost. Cut flowers wouldn't mean as much to Becky as this gorgeous plant whose name she most likely couldn't pronounce.

"Happy anniversary, Becky," Harmony said, popping up from in front of the desk.

Becky cried out, and then laughed. "Thank you, Harmony. And thank you so much for the plant."

Harmony, a pretty woman with honey-colored curls and hazel eyes, stepped around the desk and wrapped Becky in a hug. Becky's eyes pricked with hot tears as Harmony released her.

"Five years, girl." Harmony shook her head with a grin. "I can hardly believe it."

"You've worked here longer than that."

"True." Harmony laughed lightly. "But your pretty little face was here when I started."

Becky smiled. "I was just a volunteer then."

"And well on her way to running the place," Dr. Robbins said as he joined them.

Becky flushed at the man's praise. "Thanks, Doc."

He smiled down at her, warmth in his green eyes. As usual, his glasses were perched on top of his balding head and his gray hair was a little mussed.

"As our MVP, it's only fitting that you be the one to welcome the newest addition to our little family," he said.

The glass front doors slid open then and a guy entered the reception area. He was tall, with crisp chinos on his long legs. And he filled out his flannel shirt very nicely, too. A dusting of dark stubble covered his chiseled jawline. One look into his blue eyes, though? Recognition struck her hard, and old hurts followed swiftly on its heels.

"Bugs!" she said.

He smiled that familiar, slightly crooked smile, and her silly heart fluttered.

"Hey, Becks."

***

Nate Bauer stared at Becky Rollins, seeing both the pretty teenager she'd been and the gorgeous woman she was now. There was still a freshness about her that he remembered, from her rich red waves to her bright brown eyes.

They gazed at each other for a long minute.

"Bugs?" Dr. Robbins asked.

"Becks?" Harmony, the plant conservationist, asked.

A pink blush spread over Becky's fair skin, and Nate managed to nod at his new boss.

"Becky and I went to Cypress Corners High together, Dr. Robbins."

Becky swallowed audibly and nodded. "Y-yes, but Nate was a couple of years ahead of me."

That was true. She might have been younger but that

hadn't made her any less dangerous. He'd been drawn to her back then, and only the fear of losing control had kept him from doing anything more than make out with her a couple of times. A couple of amazing times, except for that last night together. He'd nearly made a mess of both of their lives before running away like a mad hornet was after him.

"It's Becky's five-year anniversary today," Harmony told him.

"Congratulations," he said to Becky.

She dipped her head, her full lips pressed shut.

"Claire made a cake, Becky," Harmony said.

That brought a bright smile to Becky's face. "Oh, yay! I was hoping for one of her cakes." She winked. "Don't tell Caro."

Harmony and Dr. Robbins laughed, but Becky's meaning was lost on Nate. He smiled anyway, feeling a little bit like a doofus.

"Nate, why don't we go into my office?" Dr. Robbins asked.

Relief flooding him, Nate nodded. "Save me some of that cake," he said to Becky.

She lost her smile and gave him a solemn nod. Harmony

turned a quizzical look in his direction, which he chose to ignore. Following Dr. Robbins, he left the reception area and was soon settled in the director's office.

"Have a seat, Nate." Dr. Robbins sat behind his paper-littered desk. "I'm very excited for you to come on."

"I'm excited to be here, sir."

The other man's eyes twinkled. "Then why did you refuse me no less than two times before?"

Nate found a smile. "I guess you wore me down, Doc."

Robbins laughed. He moved the papers about on the top of the desk, clearly seeing a pattern or system that Nate couldn't decipher. Tapping the top of his head, the director brought his glasses down to rest on his nose.

"Now, you'll be working with Harmony and Ty Walsh. Keeping the plants and animals of Cypress Corners safe is our number one priority."

Nate knew that Ty was the wildlife tech for Cypress. He nodded. "Yet pest control is a concern."

"Indeed. I read your paper on natural pesticide combinations as well as less invasive practices, and I must say I was impressed. You were wasted working for the county, if I may say so."

Nate knew better than to burn any bridges, but his work for Osceola County had been dull even for him. "I pushed a lot more papers than I thought I would."

"Yes, no worries about that now. You'll be hands-on here in Cypress."

That pleased Nate. He could use the challenge. He'd earned his master's degree from the University of Florida, after finishing his undergrad there. He was the only entomologist on staff at the Institute. He respected the place in the ecosystem for insects, but he also knew a community like Cypress Corners had to appeal to humans too. There was the seemingly-innate desire for rolling green lawns that he would never understand.

"I'm looking forward to it, sir."

"Get with Becky, Nate."

His belly clenched. "Becky?"

"Yes. She's the heart of this place. She coordinates everyone's schedules and arranges the eco-tours."

Nate cleared his throat. "Of course."

"She'll see you set up in your office, and arrange your schedule."

Nate nodded.

"You'll start with a more in-depth eco-tour with Ty this morning," Dr. Robbins went on. "And you'll want to take a tour at the Sales Center sometime this week."

Nate smiled. "I've taken one of those, sir. My mother wants to move into the Active Adult community."

"Oh?" Dr. Robbins brightened. "That would be wonderful. Then you'll have to live out here, too."

Nate shook his head. "I'm not sure about that."

The other man pursed his lips, his eyes shrewd and bright. "It happens to us all, Nate," he finally said.

"What's that?"

"You come out here and fall in love."

An image of Becky popped into Nate's head, with memories of stolen kisses and big brown eyes. "Love?"

"With Cypress, yes." The director stood. "This place has a way of getting to you."

Nate came to his feet. "I'll keep an eye out, then."

The director laughed, holding out his hand. "Welcome aboard."

Nate shook the doc's hand and left his office. He approached the reception area, steeling himself for another encounter with Becky Rollins. She was studying her computer screen, biting her full lower lip as her brows drew together. She was a little curvier than he remembered, and her soft-looking shirt didn't do much to hide her assets. He took a deep breath to dispel those inappropriate thoughts and cleared his throat.

She turned, and then her eyes went wide. "Oh!" That blush stained her smooth cheeks again and she squared her shoulders. "What can I do for you, Bugs?"

He chuckled. "I haven't been called that in years."

She smiled. "I'm sorry. Mr. Bauer."

"Nate is fine," he said. "The doc says you can show me to my office?"

She jumped to her feet and came around her desk. "You're down here by Ty's office."

Without another word, she took quick strides down the hallway to the right. He easily kept up with her, acknowledging that he wasn't above admiring her butt in those khaki shorts. She stopped short in an open doorway, causing him to bump into her. The top of her head tucked under his chin, fitting her body close to his. Her sweet scent, something like wildflowers, tickled his nose. It was delicious, and very familiar.

Placing his hands on her arms, he took a step back from her. "Sorry."

She looked at him over one shoulder and waved a hand. "No worries."

Her voice was a little bit husky. Her big eyes had flecks of gold, too. He'd forgotten that. Looking past her into the office, he let out a whistle. The room had a large desk much like the director's, and a plush looking chair behind it. A wide window behind it overlooked a courtyard bracketed by flowering trees.

"This is pretty sweet."

She walked over to the window. "You have a nice view, Nate."

He couldn't help but run his eyes over her. "That I do."

She turned to him, her eyes wide, and then laughed lightly. "Bugs Bauer, you've gotten some game since I saw you last."

"Not really, no." He rubbed a hand over the back of his neck, the skin suddenly prickly and hot. "Sorry to be inappropriate."

"No worries. We were friends back then, remember?"

Were they? He wasn't so sure about that. He

remembered thinking about her in a way he'd never thought about any of his other friends. Hell, he hadn't even thought of Laura the way he'd thought about Becky.

"Okay, thanks."

They shared another of those long looks. She dipped her head and walked past him into the hallway.

"Settle in, Bugs. Your log-in credentials are in the folder on the desk. I'll ping you when I've heard back from Ty Walsh about your eco-tour."

"Thanks, Becks."

She took an audible breath at the nickname and then left him. He sat in his new chair and spread his hands flat on his new desk. This was a new start for him. He worked for Cypress Corners now. He would prove himself worthy of the director's trust. Worthy of this new place he called home, at least figuratively.

He would just focus and not get distracted by a pretty redhead he'd thought he'd left behind years ago.

Chapter 2

Becky returned to her desk, only to find Harmony standing there. Her face was alight with open curiosity, and Becky rolled her eyes in her direction.

"Becks?" Harmony grinned. "Pretty familiar, if you ask me."

Becky snorted. "I'm not asking, thanks."

As she opened up the scheduling program, she tried to put Nate out of her head. Oh, he sure looked good.

"Becky, how well did you know Nate back then?"

Becky let out a breath and faced her friend. "Borrowing a page from Lettie's book, are you?"

Harmony laughed out loud. "Sitting under her crepe myrtle sipping sweet tea and trading gossip? Not on your life."

"That's something, then. Nate and I went to school together. Sort of. That's all."

"You really didn't know he was coming on board?"

"Nope. This might surprise you, but the doc doesn't usually clear staffing decisions with me."

Harmony shrugged. "I'm surprised to hear that, Gal Friday."

Becky found a smile. "I saw the name Bauer on some paperwork, but I didn't put two and two together."

Harmony arched a brow. "You could have gotten more than four with the electricity zinging between you two."

She snorted again. "He's engaged, Harmony. Or at least I'd heard he was a couple of years ago. He's probably married by now."

"I noticed that he's not wearing a wedding ring."

Yeah, Becky had noticed that too. "That doesn't mean anything."

Harmony held up her hands. "Okay, okay. Are you heading to the tavern for burger night tonight?"

Becky chewed on her lower lip. "I should probably skip dinner, after all that cake I plan to eat."

"Come on out, Becks."

Becky wagged a finger at her. "That had better not catch on."

"I'm just teasing you. Come on, it'll be fun. Your sister's coming."

"You spoke to Joy?"

"I tracked her down at the stables, yes."

Becky smiled. Her sister Joy had hooked up with Zach

Harris around Christmastime, and she worked with his youngest riding students when she wasn't at the community school teaching art. They were in each other's pockets, as their mother would say. They were certainly made for each other.

"I've been trying to pin her down for a girls' night, but she's been cagey."

"Then come! It won't just be a girls' night, though." Harmony winked. "Maybe your old friend will join us."

Becky growled softly. There was nothing else for it. Was she going to start avoiding places because Nate might be there? It wasn't like he was her ex or anything. She pictured those soulful blue eyes and handsome face. He'd been a hottie even back then. So he was an ex-crush. An ex-almost, maybe.

When he'd pressed against her from behind outside of his office, his chest had felt rock-hard behind her. She couldn't afford to crush on any guy right now, let alone Bugs Bauer. Her life was just about perfect, and she liked it that way.

"Oh, all right."

Harmony bobbed up and down on the toes of her hiking boots. "Good! I'll let Rick know. Now let's go eat cake!"

21

Later that afternoon, Becky went into the breakroom to box up whatever might be left of the incredible lemon-blueberry cake Claire had made. And maybe have another nibble or two. The breakroom was small, with just two round tables each with four chairs tucked beneath. A microwave and coffeemaker shared the limited counter space, but hardly anyone spent much time in here. People either went to the Town Tavern for lunch or walked over to the coffee shop or the bakery to grab a quick bite of something.

The resealable cake box sat in pride of place on top of the counter, and when she pried it open she found enough left for two good-sized pieces. There were some paper plates on the counter too, so she grabbed up the cake server and began to slice the remnant into manageable pieces.

"Is that for me?"

She glanced over her shoulder to find Nate standing in the doorway. "Didn't you get a piece earlier?"

He shook his head. "You saw my schedule, Becks. I had to ride out to the east side of the property with Ty Walsh. Then…I guess I didn't feel right just helping myself."

Taking the biggest portion she'd cut, she made him a plate. "This is for you, then. From now on, you're one of us."

He balanced the plate in one hand and grabbed a plastic fork from the counter. He took a bite, his eyes rolling skyward as he made a growl of satisfaction.

"Oh my God," he mumbled.

Becky couldn't help but laugh. "Yeah, that's about right."

He ate the piece of cake in three more bites, an expression of bliss on his handsome face.

Crossing her arms, she leaned back against the counter. "Welcome to Cypress Corners."

He grinned as he wiped his mouth. "Did this come from the bakery?"

"Nope. Claire Chapman is a phenomenal home baker, in addition to being the CPA of the development."

"Interesting. I haven't met many of the people who work across the street."

"That will change."

"Are you speaking as the girl who knows my schedule, or are you making an educated guess?"

"Both, actually. The doc and the developer often work together. The environment is key to both of them, believe it or not."

"I believe it. I read through the literature you left in my folder."

She felt a flush of pride. "I'm glad."

"Hey there, are you all set for tonight?" Harmony asked, poking her head into the breakroom. "Oh, hi Nate!"

"What's tonight?" he asked.

Becky gave a tiny shake of her head in Harmony's direction, but her friend just winked. Again.

"We're all headed to the tavern for burger night, Nate."

"Yeah?" he asked.

Becky turned wide eyes in Harmony's direction, trying her darnedest not to shake her head. *No, no, no.*

"Why don't you join us?" Harmony asked.

Becky closed her eyes and swallowed a curse.

"That sounds great," he said. "Thanks."

Becky smirked at Harmony, who waved a hand as she left the room.

"What time is dinner, Becks?"

She faced him again. Clearly, he had no idea that Harmony had more in mind for the two of them than just sharing a meal. Becky wouldn't be the one to set him straight. There was no problem, was there? She could withstand being so close to the guy she hadn't seen in years. Easy-Peasy.

"Six."

"Cool." He drew out his phone. "I'll see you then. And thanks for the cake."

She nodded mutely. As he turned away, she let out a sigh of relief. He was clearly calling his girlfriend or fiancée or whatever. Catching bits of his side of the conversation, things like "…letting you know I won't be home until later" and "…just meeting up with some people from work for dinner" confirmed that in her mind. That put him out of reach. And let her off the hook, thanks.

Her belly did that silly trembly thing again, and she left the breakroom. She would put on her big-girl panties and go dinner with Bugs and her friends. How hard could it be?

***

How hard could it be? Nate pocketed his phone and turned to find Becky gone. He could breathe a little bit easier now, at least. Now that she wasn't so close to him in the tiny breakroom. Dinner with her tonight, and a few other people thank God, shouldn't be too difficult to get through. At least he wouldn't be tempted to spread that lemon frosting all over her smooth rosy skin and lick it off.

He hadn't felt that zing of attraction in years, and he doubted he'd ever felt it for any woman but Becks. It was like all the years since they'd last seen each other hadn't even happened. That the time since he'd run away from her hadn't passed, either.

"Don't be an idiot," he mumbled to himself.

Now wasn't the time to wax nostalgic about the one that got away or whatever. Besides, he had more to worry about than overactive hormones ruining what could be a long career path at the Institute. Looking after his mother was practically a full-time job on its own.

Frowning down at his phone, he slipped it back in his pocket. Would she ever be strong enough to stand on her own two feet? Getting her moved into the Active Adult community would be the first step toward her living more independently. She had no choice in the matter. He couldn't live there with her, now could he?

"Damn straight," he said.

He went back to his office to review some of what he'd learned today. On his *first* day. It had been a pretty good one, aside from wayward thoughts of a certain redhead popping into his head. She'd come in a few times, though. She'd had to show him how to access his schedule on the closed network and a few other things throughout the day. He'd had a tough time concentrating afterwards, since she tended to leave her wildflower scent behind her.

Glancing at his phone again, he saw it was nearly six o'clock. He'd gotten lost in a report about the algae fields planned for the far east side of the property, he'd seen the designated spot on his tour with Ty Walsh, and realized now that the place was dead quiet. He shut his Institute-issued laptop and tidied his desk. After turning off the light and heading down the dim hallway, he walked out into the cool spring evening.

The twilight sky was stained a light shade of purple. The air smelled fresh, clean, and almost wet. The trees had spring green leaves on most of their branches, and it was clear to Nate that Cypress Corners would be a beautiful place in just a few weeks. The entomological residents would surge in population as well. Insects would soon swarm, insects of just about every type, and it was up to him to make sure they were kept in control.

The brick-lined walk was nearly empty, which he guessed was due to the fact that most of the businesses on the

27

square were closed for the night. The old-fashioned streetlamps buzzed on overhead as he passed beneath, and he smiled absently at an older man and woman who walked past him.

The Town Tavern was adjacent to the Clubhouse, which was more of an upscale type of restaurant. The tavern was where he'd met with Dr. Robbins last month for lunch, and it seemed to be a warm and welcoming place. He had no idea who would be there tonight, other than Becky and Harmony.

There were a few people milling around in the entry, close to the hostess stand. Nate was at a loss. He was never good in these kind of situations. He knew so few people here he felt that he stuck out like a Palmetto bug at a picnic.

"Hey, Nate!"

Nate looked over into the bar area not far from the entry to see Ty Walsh waving him over. He was smiling broadly, and Nate returned the expression and walked over to the bar.

"Hey, Ty."

Ty shook his hand and put his arm around a pretty dark-haired woman at his side. "Nate, this is my wife Cassie."

Nate dipped his head. "Pleasure to meet you."

"Hi, Nate." Cassie arched a brow in her husband's

direction. "Can I expect talk to turn to all sorts of fauna during dinner? You know, big and small?"

Ty, the wildlife tech of Cypress, chuckled. "I promised you, baby. No shop talk."

Cassie snorted, her blue eyes twinkling. "I'll believe that when I see it."

"When you see what?" another woman asked as she joined then.

Nate turned to her, seeing that she looked a lot like his Becks. He knew her from years ago. Becky's sister. "Joy?"

Joy beamed a smile. "Hi there, Bugs!"

Nate groaned. "There it is."

Joy laughed and touched his arm. "Just teasing you, Nate. Becky told me you started at the Institute today."

A tall guy stood at Joy's side, and Nick tilted his head. He looked familiar, too.

"Zach Harris," the guy said. "You're Nate Bauer. I think we played against each other in high school."

"I think we did, yeah." Nate shook his hand, too. "You played for St. Cloud."

"Baseball?" Joy asked.

"No, honey." Zach grinned. "Ping Pong."

Joy clicked her tongue. "Okay, cowboy." She turned back toward Nate. "So Nate, how was your first day?"

"Pretty great, actually," Nate said.

"Nate survived the full-on tour today," Ty put in. "We checked out where the algae fields are going, too."

Cassie wrinkled her nose. "Are there a lot of bugs around algae, Nate?"

"I wouldn't think so," he said. "Not the way these will be constructed. The water won't remain stagnant."

Cassie nodded. "So no mosquitos, then."

"Not around the algae fields, no."

"How about bees around the coffee shop?" Joy asked.

"Are bees a problem out here?" Nate asked.

"Not really," Ty said. "Yellow jackets, sure."

"*Vespula* of some kind, then," Nate said. "That makes sense. They're attracted to sweets in and around trashcans."

"Vespula?" Zach asked.

"A type of wasp."

"How do we get rid of them?" Joy asked.

"Our goal shouldn't be to get rid of them, actually," Nate said. "Keeping the areas near people free of sugars and other sweet things should discourage them from coming around."

"Makes sense," Zach said.

"They're an important predator of pest insects like flies and spiders too, not to mention fly larvae," Nate went on. He soon recognized the familiar combination of interest and revulsion stamped on their faces. He winced. "Sorry. I tend to go on sometimes."

"I remember that," Becky said as she joined them. "You're not called Bugs for nothing."

Nate turned, gut-punched as he took her in. She'd obviously gone home to change before coming to the tavern, and now she wore a long-sleeve T-shirt with a vintage Route 66 sign printed on it. The shirt was a soft rust color, a shade or two darker than her hair which was loose from its earlier ponytail and wavy now. The worn jeans hugged her curves, and the black Chuck Taylors on her feet were sexy somehow.

"Hey, Becks."

Becky rolled her pretty eyes and her sister laughed.

Chapter 3

Harmony and Rick Chapman walked in then, and Becky used their entrance as an excuse to step away from Nate. She could smell his spicy outdoorsy scent and, taken with that sheepish expression on his face after he'd schooled them all about yellow jackets—oh, those eyes of his—she'd wanted to give him a hug.

She waved to Harmony, hoping to cover the blush heating her cheeks at the thought of just where that hug might lead. Goodness knew it had happened before. Eons ago.

"They've set the big table near the fireplace for us," Harmony said as she came close and gave Becky a hug. She turned to her husband. "Rick, this is—"

"Nate Bauer, I know." Rick held out his hand. "Mr. Forbes is pleased you've come on board at the Institute." He tilted his head toward his wife. "I'd say he's nearly as excited as the doc."

Nate smiled and nodded. "I'm really glad to be here."

They all exchanged more greetings and then made their way over to the round table near the fireplace and bank of windows. The view of the golf course was stellar, but at this time of day it was dark and muted.

"Did you know Zach and Nate played baseball against each other, Becky?" Joy asked as they all took their seats.

"Oh?"

"Back in the day," Zach put in.

She sure remembered how cute Bugs had looked in his uniform back in the day, all right. She looked around the table, seeing that she had no chance of sitting anywhere but next to Nate. Everyone was paired up, so she let out a breath and settled in the chair next to him. Their knees touched of course, seeing as the table was round. His hair, thick and a rich brown color, caught some gold from the shaded overhead lights. He'd rolled up his sleeves at some point in the day, and his forearms looked nice and strong. She kept her hands on her lap to keep from giving him a little pinch for old time's sake.

The tavern was decorated a lot like an English pub, with dark wood furniture and paneling, green-shaded lamps and lots of brass. It was one of her favorite places in Cypress, aside from the killer coffee shop and yummy bakery.

A server she didn't know well came to the table and everyone ordered their drinks and meals. Conversation was lively all around the table, but Becky noticed that Nate was his familiar quiet self. His gaze was on the table as he fiddled with the edge of his napkin. After a long minute, he slid his eyes in her direction.

"This might sound like a line, but do you come here often?" Nate asked her.

"Yep, I do. Their pizza is surprisingly delicious, but tonight it's all burgers all the time."

"They deliver," Harmony said. "Room service. Sort of."

His brows drew together and his face took on that thinking expression that was cute and a little bit hot. "Not out to St. Cloud, I'll bet."

"Nope." Harmony answered. "Sorry."

"Are you going to move out here, Nate?" her sister Joy asked.

Nate blinked, his thick lashes hiding his eyes for a moment. "I don't think so. I'm not sure."

That was a weird answer, but Becky wasn't going to push him for more. Drinks and then burgers arrived, and she chose to focus on her meal and not on the man sitting quietly beside her.

The party, so to speak, broke up just after seven thirty. Nate walked her out, and she was sure that would spark new talk tomorrow. He had looked so clueless when she'd joined them all earlier, with his ruddy cheeks and sheepish expression. She hadn't been kidding him earlier. He always seemed to lose himself when he was talking about bugs. It was kind of icky, but in an adorable sort of way.

They all stepped outside onto the wide concrete steps in front of the tavern. There was a touch of a chill in the air, but her long-sleeve T was enough. She should have driven back to the square when she'd gone home to change, though. That would have been the smarter thing, but she'd ridden her bike home in the dark lots of times.

"See you tomorrow, Becky," Harmony said.

Becky gave her friend a little wave and smiled at her husband. "Sure."

Joy gave her a hug, grinning as she pulled back. "'Night, sis."

She leveled a look at her sister. "'Night."

Joy laughed but Zach held up both hands in apparent surrender as they headed out. Cassie Walsh was clearly holding back a smile as she and Ty left, dipping her head as the two of them descended the steps. Becky growled softly to herself. *With friends like these…*

"So you live in here?" he asked. "In Cypress?"

She nodded. "I do. I have a condo not far from the town square."

He stuck his hands in his front pockets. "I'm in St. Cloud now."

"You used to live south of the high school, right?"

His gaze slid away. "Yeah. We lived with my mother's brother back then."

She tried to recall anything else about his home life from the time she knew him before, but drew a blank. They began to walk toward the Institute, silent together for a few minutes.

"You survived your first day, Nate." She nudged him with her shoulder. "What do you think of it?"

"Dr. Robbins is great," he said. "Just looking over the land surveys and the planned expansions tells me that the Institute will be pretty busy."

"It's always been that way."

They stopped and sat down on a metal bench not far from the Institute. It was like many of the benches in Cypress, part seating/part sculpture. This one resembled a dragon fly. She was very comfortable with him, which shouldn't be possible. True, she'd known him when they were teenagers. She'd made out with him, for goodness sake. Now, though? He was the hot new guy and yet at the same time he was simply Bugs Bauer.

"So are you going to move out here?" she asked.

He shrugged one of his broad shoulders. "I don't know. I want to get my mother into the Active Adult section. I think it would be good for her."

"She lives with you?"

He gave her a crooked smile. "Thanks for putting it that way. Yeah, she does."

"How does she get along with your girlfriend?"

His brows rose. "What girlfriend?"

"I thought…" She bit her bottom lip. "Earlier, Nate. When you were on your phone. I assumed you were talking to your girlfriend about your change of plans or something."

"Nope." He shook his head. "No girlfriend."

She nodded, staring up at the dark clear sky. They grew quiet again, but it felt more like a cocoon than a rope wrapped around them. It was intimate somehow.

"I'd heard you'd gotten engaged," she said.

His lips thinned, and then he ran a hand over his hair. "I

did. Nearly got married, too."

Whoa. There was a story there. And from the clouds in those blue eyes of his it wasn't one he wanted to share. Heck, she wasn't sure she wanted to hear it. The cocoon suddenly felt stifling.

She was never good at this sort of stuff. She'd had one boyfriend in college and dated a little bit on and off afterwards, but there hadn't been anyone in so long. True, she'd been romanced and then dumped by Kent the Slug about a year and a half ago. She didn't pine for the golf pro, and she sure as heck didn't miss him. Nate, though? She'd fallen for him in high school and if he kept up this aw-shucks attitude that seemed to cling to him she was in great danger of falling again.

Coming to her feet, she rubbed her hands over her jeans. "I should get home."

***

Nate stood too, looking around. "Where's your car?"

"I rode my bicycle. I usually do."

"You're going to ride home in the dark?"

"I don't live very far."

He shook his head. "Let me take you home."

38

"And how will I get my bike? No. That's sweet of you to offer, but no."

"Sweet?" He huffed out a breath. "I guess, but I can easily put your bike in the back of my truck."

"Okay." She was very still for a second. "Thanks."

They walked toward the back of the Institute, and to him it felt like there was no one else in the world at the moment. Or in Cypress Corners, in any event. He could hear the distinctive trill of several Southeastern field crickets coming from deep within the clumps of ornamental grasses lining one side of the walkway.

She stopped when they came to where his truck was parked and slid him a smile. "Yeah, you can easily put my bike back there."

The big Silverado had been his one and only indulgence after Laura had broken up with him. He'd told himself he needed it for his work with the county, but it was nice to have something of his own that he'd never shared with his ex.

Becky unlocked her cute little sherbet-colored bicycle while he let down the tailgate. He lifted the bike easily and set it carefully in the back. She paused and bit that full lower lip of hers, he remembered that she'd often done that, and then climbed up into the cab.

He got in and started the truck, and then turned to her. "Just tell me where."

She directed him toward the townhouses set not far from the square. "My place is toward the back of this block."

"I haven't seen much of Cypress since I decided to take the job." He steered westward. "These townhouses are nice."

"Jessie and Noah Brady live in this one on the corner," she said as he drove past. "And Eli and Caro Graham, she runs the bakery we were talking about, live in the other end unit."

He nodded absently, certain he could listen to the sound of her voice all night. Her scent reached him in the closeness of the cab, and for a second he longed to close his eyes and just breathe her in. He remembered reading that scent was most closely tied to memories. He sure was thinking about the times they'd spent together years ago. The kisses. The petting. He might have just been a horny teenager but even then he knew there was more to Becky Rollins than just the expectation of a good time. Maybe that was why he'd run from her after they'd nearly taken things too far.

"We're almost there," she said, breaking through to

him. "Take a right at the next stop sign."

He nodded again and she pointed out her condo. The two-story building was clearly made up of stacked one-floor units, but the style was keeping in line with the townhouses in the same village with its wide moldings and deep eaves. Each building was painted in a different shade of either green or tan and trimmed with white, but he couldn't see much more than that at this time of night.

"These look nice, too."

She lifted her chin a little. "They are, and I finally have my own place."

"Where did you live before?" He squeezed the wheel a little. "With a boyfriend?"

To his surprise and relief, she laughed. "No. I lived at the Cypress Inn. My mother runs it."

He'd seen the inn, of course. It was one of the largest free-standing buildings aside from the Sales Center and Institute.

"That big Victorian-looking house out by the main lakeshore, right?"

"That's the place. My parents bought it and moved us all in right before Joy and I started high school."

"You lived in the inn? I don't think I knew that."

"It's not as weird as it sounds. The family has a separate area. It wasn't separate enough for me, though."

"As an only child of a single mother, I'll just have to take your word on that."

She nodded.

"Yet you're still in Cypress," he said.

"This place was my parents' dream, but it caught me too."

He parked the truck in the driveway she indicated behind her building and put it in park. "It's a nice place, Cypress."

He suspected that he sounded like he was either trying to talk himself into it or out of it. Maybe Becky might be able to help him figure that out, but not tonight.

He shut off the engine and got out. She was quick, and was out of the truck before he could walk around and open the door for her. It wasn't like this was a date, so he was glad she'd saved him from that embarrassment.

He lifted her bike out of the truck and set it on the concrete. She tucked her helmet underneath her arm and pushed a button on her key fob that lifted the garage door.

She wheeled her bike just inside the garage, and then faced him.

That feeling of closeness struck him, something he hadn't felt in a long damn time. She was so sweet, too. Funny and warm. Suddenly the thought of heading back to St. Cloud to the cluttered house he shared with his mother depressed him.

"Well," she said, staring up at him.

Her lips were shiny, her eyes deep, and he didn't want to leave her. Everything seemed to fall away in that second: his new job, his mother, his past. There was nothing but Becks and he couldn't resist the temptation she posed.

Leaning toward her, he buzzed a quick kiss on her lips. She made a soft sound of surprise as her lips parted. He straightened, fighting the urge to kiss her crazy right there on the driveway. Even that slight touch had filled his mouth with a hot sweetness.

"Good night, Becks."

She blinked and gave him a smile, she had a gorgeous smile, and nodded. "Good night, Bugs."

As he made the fifteen minute drive into St. Cloud, he breathed in her wildflower scent that lingered in the truck cab.

He was torn between hoping the truck would still smell like her in the morning and hoping that he wouldn't have a tangible reminder of a life he could never have.

He'd have to get his *own* life before he could even consider anything more, and he was damned if he could figure out how to do that.

Chapter 4

"Rise and shine, Nate honey!"

His mother's singsong voice reached down the short hallway between the living area and in through his open bedroom door. Groaning, he sat up and rubbed his hands over his face. He'd had some very vivid, and very hot, dreams last night starring Becks. He couldn't go there. They were co-workers now, and it would serve him well to keep that in mind. To keep his focus. He'd managed to for the past three days. Since their kiss, anyway.

He crossed to the doorway. "Thanks, Mom. I'm up."

He closed the door and went into his bathroom. Once he was showered and dressed, he joined his mother in the kitchen. She was singing softly as she brewed him a cup of coffee. She wore what he was coming to think of as her uniform since she'd retired from her job as a bank teller. Crisply-ironed jeans and a long-sleeve buttoned shirt. Today's was bright pink, and her cheeks were nearly the same color. Her chin-length hair, thick and the same dark brown as his, was pulled back with a headband. He braced himself for what he suspected was coming, judging by her mood.

"What's up?" he asked.

She clasped her hands together. "Nate, I think I met the one!"

He held his staid expression. He couldn't count the number of times he'd heard her say the very same thing. It seemed to be for as long as he could remember.

"Oh?" He kept his tone even. "When did this happen?"

"Last night at the movies." She poured some cream into his coffee. "You know how they have discount seats on Mondays at the theater downtown? That's the night they show those classic romantic comedies I love."

He stirred his coffee. "Sure."

"I went alone, which you know isn't something I like to do. But my friend Linda was busy with her grandbabies."

He lifted his coffee cup to his lips and slowly sipped. He knew there was no need to make any sort of answer. Not when she was in middle of a meet-cute story.

"So I'm sitting in the theater, in the center as I like to do." She set a plate of round toasted waffles, dressed with butter and syrup, in front of him. "There were empty seats on either side of me, even long into the previews."

He nodded and began to eat his breakfast.

"Then, during the opening credits, a charming

gentleman sat next to me! His name is Charles, but he likes to be called Chip."

"Like the chipmunk?

She blinked at him, and then laughed. "No, silly! He's very distinguished. I would put his age at around sixty. He bought me a box of Snowcaps, you know how much I love Snowcaps, and we shared the armrest."

Nate breathed in slowly through his nose. "It sounds like you had a nice time."

"We did, we did." She sat down on the stool opposite him. "We went for coffee later at that little place next to the theater and talked and talked. I told him that I'm looking into moving to Cypress."

Nate swallowed a groan. "I'll bet he was interested."

"Oh, yes. I also told him that you and I were going to look at the place this weekend."

That, he hadn't expected. "This weekend?"

"Yes! The sooner I get settled in, the sooner Chip can visit me."

Nate wiped his mouth with a napkin and set it down beside his empty plate. "I guess we can go take a tour on Saturday."

Her eyes, as blue as his own, sparkled. "Wonderful!"

She picked up his plate and mug, and then set them in the sink. "Hurry on out to that Institute of yours, Nate. It would never do for you to come to work late in your first week."

He took a breath and came to his feet. "Thanks for breakfast, Mom."

He kissed her offered cheek and she smiled up at him. "Love you, Nate."

"Love you, Mom."

He stepped outside of the little rental house they shared, a sense of urgency dogging his heels. His mother was going to fall for this Chip, and then the guy would most likely want to move into her place in Cypress.

"Not if I have anything to say about it," he grumbled as he got into his truck. He could take his Snowcaps and his armrest and prey on some other unsuspecting woman.

Nate had scrimped and saved over the past five years, and he had both a nice nest egg for himself and enough money for a considerable down payment for his mom's place. From what he'd seen so far, the Active Adult community was a hit and any investment they might make would see an increase in value over time.

When he parked his truck behind the Institute, five minutes before the nine o'clock hour, he saw that Becky's bike was already attached to the rack. The sky above was clogged with thick gray clouds, and he wouldn't be surprised if they got some rain today. Making a mental note to check the weather app when he got to his desk, he locked the truck and entered the building through the back.

The pretty little redhead was seated at her desk, which was already a flurry of activity judging by the lights on her phone and the speed of her fingers on the computer keyboard. He stepped forward to say hello when he was waylaid by Harmony Chapman.

"Good morning, Nate."

He turned and smiled at her. "Good morning."

"Becky is a little busy, so I thought I'd tell you that Rick is expecting you at the Sales Center today."

"Really?" He drew out his phone and checked his schedule. Sure enough, he'd been pinged by Becks and the meeting with Rick Chapman was scheduled for nine thirty today, Thursday. "Thanks."

She was watching him, her eyes going from him to

Becky and back, until she smiled again and walked back toward her office. As he was turning toward his own, Becky called out to him.

He looked over at her. "Hey, Becks."

She flashed him a smile, tucking a lock of hair behind one ear. "Hey, Bugs. I pinged you."

He nodded. "Yeah, I have a meeting with Rick Chapman."

Her brows rose, and then she smiled a little easier. She lowered her voice. "Um, thanks again for the ride home the other night."

"Any time."

He stood there like a doofus, just like he had that first morning. Dipping his head again, he left her to go hide in his office. He did have to check the weather app, after all.

If he had to make the forecast? He'd call it cloudy with a chance of trouble.

***

Becky watched Nate's long easy strides as he made his way down the hall toward his office. She'd seen the schedule changes come through, and couldn't ignore the little jolt of electricity she'd felt as she'd read his name. That same electricity seemed to crackle in the air between them, especially after their almost-kiss that night. All right, it was a kiss. She shouldn't dwell on it, though. They were co-workers. Old friends, she guessed.

"Cool your jets, Becks," she murmured.

Harmony just happened to be in earshot for that little gem. She let out a short laugh as she sailed on past her toward the director's office. Becky scowled at her, which just made Harmony's smile widen.

Giving herself a mental shake, she set Bugs Bauer out of her mind and opened up her emails. There were several regarding the upcoming Spring Festival. It was high time she reviewed the plans. Easter has come and gone, so Cypress had to find something to fill the time until Flag Day. She was only half-kidding. Cypress Corners might as well be called "the town afraid to be bored."

As the director's go-to girl, it was on her shoulders to represent the Institute at the festival meetings. Her duties for the last event, up to and including making sure every last piece of Easter candy had been found and/or removed from the green on the town square, had kept her busy. That would most likely explain why she'd been too distracted to realize that Nate was the Bauer coming on board this week. That was her story and she was sticking with it.

The Spring Festival would involve a lot more than the kids' egg hunt had. The Institute would have a booth, of course. Something with to do with conservation. Maybe she should get with Harmony and pick her brain. It was planting season, and visitors and residents should be reminded about using native plants and not choosing anything invasive. Suddenly, something came to her and she snapped her fingers.

"Lettie!" she said aloud.

Charlotte Fairfax, Lettie to everyone who knew her in Cypress Corners, was the unofficial authority on all things that grew. She was famous for her plant knowledge, which rivaled even Harmony's. Plus she was a hoot. She said outrageous things, even borderline racy things, and could totally get away with them. She was a self-described "woman of a certain age," and Southern gentility clung to her like Spanish moss on a live oak.

Checking her schedule again, Becky entered a meeting with the woman on festival business. She would head to the coffee shop for lunch. Gracie always had some snacks on hand to purchase in addition to the best coffee east of Orlando. Then Becky would corner the woman in the courtyard.

Drawing her small tablet out of her bag, she made some notes. If she could manage to get Lettie to man the Institute's booth, the doc would be thrilled. He always seemed a little shy around Lettie, which was endearing. The man was a widower, and his daughter was busy with her family up in Orlando. Becky never traded in gossip, something decidedly different from Lettie's m.o. Still, she believed the doc's daughter was having marital troubles.

Lettie could usually be found in her favorite spot beneath the branches of a crepe myrtle tree. Becky reasoned that maybe she should stop at the bakery first. No one could say no to Caro's lemon lavender scones. Pleased to have a course of action, she hummed to herself as she returned her attention to the director's appointments along with those of the rest of the people at the Institute.

She lingered on Nate's name again, feeling a little silly. "Why don't I just scribble his name in my notebook?" she chided herself as she clicked through to the rest of the morning's activities.

A clap of thunder all but shook the wide front windows, and Becky jumped in her seat. Then she noticed how dark the sky had become. Her spirits sinking, she began to rethink her assault on Lettie today.

The double doors whooshed open and a drenched Nate hurried inside. His hair was plastered onto his forehead and his camp shirt looked soaked through.

"Bugs!" She grabbed one of the folded towels kept behind the reception desk and handed it to him. "Here. You're soaked."

"Thanks." He began to rub the towel over his head. "I should have taken my jacket, but I figured since my meeting was only across the street…"

"That was your first mistake."

He lowered the towel and she was tempted to smooth down his messy waves herself. She stepped back behind her desk, putting some well-needed distance between the two of them. He went back toward the glass doors, staring up at the darkened sky.

"Doesn't look like it's going to let up any time soon."

"I know."

He must have caught the touch of regret in her voice,

because he turned back to her. "Did you have an outdoor tour planned today?"

"No, nothing like that."

"Then what's wrong, Becks?"

She studied him for a second, then shrugged. "I'm in charge of the Institute's role in the Spring Festival."

"Ah. I think the blond guy across the street was talking about that."

"Oliver, yes. He's the point person for the Sales Center, I think."

"What all is involved?"

She smiled. "Are you looking to lend a helping hand, Bugs?"

He shrugged. "Maybe. If it's nothing too scary."

"Scary?" She puffed out a breath. "You wrangle wasps and spiders all day. What's more scary than that?"

"Wrangling is a stretch, but I'll give you that."

She tapped her chin. "You know, I just might take you up on that."

He handed her the towel. "Thanks, again. I'll see you later."

"Nate, wait." He turned back to her, his brows raised.

"Want to join me for lunch? I was thinking of grabbing something from the bakery and then heading to the coffee shop."

His brows drew together for a second, and then he nodded. "Sure." He dropped a wink. "Ping me."

She waved a hand and grabbed her tablet again. If she knew Lettie, and after more than ten years she knew Lettie, the woman wouldn't be able to refuse her request. Not if it came from handsome nature expert Bugs Bauer, that was.

Her spirits much lighter than the weather outside might elicit, she planned her attack. She would have to get through another close encounter with Nate, but she was big girl. She hadn't let the mess with Kent interfere with her work, and she wouldn't let her infatuation with Bugs do so either.

That was her story, and she was sticking with it.

Chapter 5

Nate left his office, bound once again for the reception area. He'd learned from his visit to the Sales Center that the place, along with all of the model homes, were closed on the weekend. This seemed unusual to him but, from what he'd learned from Eli Graham, the practice didn't seem to affect sales in the community. In fact, that built-in family time seemed to attract buyers. It did put a crimp in his Saturday plans, however. Maybe he could talk to the doc and carve out a little time on Monday to tour the Active Adult section with his mother.

When he reached Becky's desk, he found her tapping furiously at her keyboard, that plump lower lip of hers caught tight in her teeth. He studied her profile for a second, her flawless skin, and then cleared his throat.

She turned to him, and then her eyes rounded and her mouth curved into a smile. "Bugs." She came to her feet and slipped into the jacket hanging on the back of her chair, turning a frown toward the wet and darkened landscape visible outside the front doors. "I'd hoped the rain would have let up by now."

"I won't melt." Nate shrugged. "Like my mother says, I

might be sweet but I'm not made of sugar."

She laughed. "That's a new one on me. Sounds like something Lettie might say."

Nate had heard that Lettie woman's name mentioned, always accompanied by a smile or a suggestive brow lift. "If you say so."

He grabbed an umbrella from the stand near the front door. It was a big one, a green and white golf-style deal with the Cypress Institute logo on every other panel. The doors opened and he waved Becky ahead of him and opened the umbrella.

The rain was wind-driven, and they stood very close together as they made their way over the wet brick walk.

"Bakery first," she said, her shoulder tucked tightly against him.

He followed her lead and pulled open the door, hearing the five-note chime of a pop song he recognized. "Sweet escape," he said.

"That's what they tell me," a pretty blond woman said as she wiped down the closest table, the only one not occupied at the moment. "Hey there, Becky. Nate."

"Hi, Caro," Nate said.

"You know Caro?" Becky asked.

"Her husband Eli introduced us earlier today," he said.

"I made an emergency run to the Sales Center this morning," Caro said. "Apparently their coffee maker gave up the ghost."

"Horrors." Becky laughed. "Caro, this is kind of an emergency, too."

Caro nodded. "What do you need?"

"Three of your lemon lavender scones."

While Caro hurried back behind the counter to fill their order, Nate looked around the place. It was crowded, which was no surprise given the time and the weather. The woman's husband had spoken of his wife and her bakery, pride in his voice, and Nate had to admit it did look pretty sweet. No pun intended.

Becky soon held the bright green bag tightly in her hands. "Okay, on to the coffee shop."

"That's lunch?"

Becky shook her head. "Lunch later. Mission first."

Her eyes sparkled and Nate wondered just what she'd gotten him into. "Mission?"

"Operation Get Lettie."

"For the festival?" Caro asked.

Becky nodded vigorously. "Yep. Wish us luck!"

"You got it."

Nate dutifully opened the umbrella as soon as they stepped back outside. "To the coffee shop, Becks."

Her face was dewy with raindrops and her hair curled around her face. She looked adorable and hot. "Onward, Bugs."

The coffee shop wasn't far, so he held the door open and the umbrella high as she entered the place. He followed, and then bent to place his mouth near her ear. "What's my role here?"

She leaned back, pressing against his chest. "Just follow my lead," she stage-whispered out of the side of her mouth. "There she is."

He soon saw their objective, sitting at a table set in one corner of the coffee shop. The place was as crowded as the bakery had been, but the older woman appeared to be sitting alone with a cup of coffee at her elbow and an assortment of magazines spread out on the table.

"Lettie!" Becky called as they approached.

"Hello there, Becky Rollins." The woman eyed Nate for

a long second. "And I believe this is the latest young gentleman to arrive in Cypress Corners?"

Nate bobbed his chin. "Nate Bauer, ma'am."

"Oh, another southerner? How divine."

"Born and raised right here," he said.

"Well, well. And here I thought Becky's sweet sister had grabbed a hold of the last southern gentleman to be seen around these parts."

"Nate this is Charlotte Fairfax. Zach and Nate actually know each other, Lettie," Becky said. She appeared nervous to Nate, shifting her feet and fiddling with the bottom ties of her rain jacket. "Fancy seeing you here."

"Now, Becky." The older woman clicked her tongue. "Nate, our dear girl here is alluding to the fact that I am quite often a fixture here on the town square. Sadly, the rain has drooped my favorite crepe myrtle and made my usual table uninhabitable this afternoon."

"I'm sorry to hear that," Nate said.

By the sparkle in the woman's eyes beneath the silvery fringe of bangs, he quickly caught on to his particular role in Becky's objective. Lettie was apparently a practiced flirt. She wore a thick nubby sweater over a flowered smock, and by

61

the bright green crocs on her feet, she was clearly more accustomed to being outside.

"Nate and I were just going to grab a couple of drinks, Lettie. May we get you something?"

Lettie shook her head and held her cardboard cup aloft. "Not at the moment, thank you. Sipping on orange blossom tea today, Becky dear. Seems the right season for it, doesn't it Nate?"

The aromatic tea was something his mother might drink, so he smiled his agreement. Lettie batted her lashes and slid her gaze to Becky once more.

"Now, I know you and your gentleman didn't come here just to get out of the rain."

Becky's cheeks turned red but Nate held his expression.

"We picked up some of Sweet Escape's lemon lavender scones, Lettie. Three, to be precise."

Lettie clasped her hands. "Oh, a decadent lunch? Please join me at my rainy day table."

Nate watched as Becky squared her shoulders. They joined Lettie, and Becky didn't wait before going forward with her request.

"Lettie, you might know that I'm handling the

Institute's role regarding the Spring Festival."

"I do indeed." Lettie leaned her crossed arms on the tabletop. "Dear girl, you know you have but to ask what is clearly on the tip of your tongue."

Becky turned an anxious gaze in Nate's direction, so he picked up the ball. "Ms. Fairfax, it would be a great honor and an enormous help if you would assist us with our booth at the festival."

Lettie's smile widened. "Lettie, please. Nate, it would be my honor to spread my love of plants and Cypress Corners by doing my own little part."

Becky let out a yelp of excitement, bounding out of her chair to wrap her arms around the older woman. Lettie laughed, as she hugged her back just as fiercely.

"Thank you so much, Lettie!" Becky blew out a breath, her eyes bright. "This is just fantastic."

Lettie nodded. "Now, Nate. Do me a favor?"

"Anything, ma'am."

"Take this girl to a real lunch?" She grabbed onto the green bag from the bakery and slid it closer to herself. "I will, however, keep these scones for myself."

Nate came to his feet, bowing slightly to her. "That is a

very good idea. Come on, Becks."

Lettie's brows arched at the nickname, and Nate briefly wondered if he would pay for that slip.

"Right behind you, Bugs."

And there it is. Chuckling, he led Becky out into the rain again.

***

"The tavern?" Nate asked her.

"Sounds good." She rolled her neck to release the lingering tension. "I can't believe how smoothly that went."

"Lettie clearly loves you, Becks."

Warmth filled her and she dipped her head. "I've known her since we moved here."

"Familiarity doesn't necessarily equal affection."

She blinked. "That's a little deep for a rainy afternoon."

He chuckled again, that rumble she really liked. "It's a little perfect, I think. And something I've been telling my mother for years."

"Is she a romantic?"

"A hopeless one, yes. Falls in love at the sight of a smile."

His expression was shuttered now. She used the rain as

an excuse to cut their conversation short on the walk to the tavern. They ordered a couple of slices of pizza at the bar and then she began to flesh out her ideas for the festival booth.

"Plants and animals, of course." She sipped at her diet soda, warming to her topic. "Ty will consult, and hopefully give a talk."

"Hopefully?" He arched one brow. "More scones?"

She laughed lightly. "No, he'll be all in. Worse comes to worst, I'll just have his wife Cassie lean on him. He can't say no to her."

He wiped his mouth and nodded. "I assume Harmony will handle plants?"

"Yep. So it will fall to you to be our bug guy. You'll give a talk as well, won't you? Something about healthy pest management maybe?"

"Whatever you need, Becks."

She shouldn't, but she sure liked when he called her that. "Thanks so much for all of this, Nate. Facing Lettie takes a certain amount of bravery."

"She's a character, to be sure."

"She's a dear, but she has a certain way about her. I thought you would be just the thing to get her over on my

65

side."

"You needed me for my body." He winked. "I have no problem with that."

"Lettie is a sucker for a pretty face."

He smiled and dug into his second slice. He did look pretty nice sitting there, his damp hair curling over his forehead and his cheeks ruddy. She was feeling much too comfortable much too fast, but she wouldn't worry about that now. He wasn't giving off any sort of hook-up vibe, despite that kiss they'd shared the other night. She would take her cue from him and keep their relationship friendly.

The rain didn't let up as the afternoon wore on. As she was closing down her computer, Harmony popped up at her desk.

"So what about Sunday?" she asked.

Becky tilted her head. "What's Sunday?"

Harmony shook her head. "Like you don't know. Our barbecue, of course. Rick isn't very happy if a weekend goes by without his getting a chance to cook meat with fire. We'd love to have you."

The Chapmans' weekend barbecues were indeed legendary. Their house, situated across from the main lakeshore, was the perfect spot for friends and family to gather. She'd attended many of them over the years, of course. She was never one to overstay her welcome, however. As the Chapman clan grew, with spouses and babies added to the group, Becky had pulled back a little. Besides, her mother liked to do a Sunday family dinner now and again.

"If you're sure it won't be a bother?"

Harmony shook her head. "Never. It's been weeks since we've gotten you over to the house."

"Then I'd love to come."

Harmony's eyes began to twinkle. "Good."

Becky leveled a look at her friend. "Harmony Chapman, what are you up to?"

Harmony gave her an innocent look that was cute but didn't fool her for a second. "Who, me?"

She turned and headed down the hallway toward Nate's office.

"Lettie 2.0," Becky murmured.

"Hey, Becks?"

Nate's voice caused her to shiver, so she braced her hands on her desk and lifted her head to face him. "What's up, Nate?"

"It's still raining."

"True. And?"

"How about I give you a ride home?"

She thought about the wisdom of being alone with him in the cab of his truck again, breathing him in and feeling his heat, and knew she should refuse. She couldn't ride her bike home, but there had to be some other way to get there, right?

"You don't have to do that."

"I know."

It was the height of foolishness to turn down his offer, even if it could be dangerous not to.

"Thanks."

"Do you want to grab dinner first?"

He looked so unsure, so endearing, that she had no real choice but to have pity on him. A little bit, anyway.

"Are you asking me on a date, Bugs?"

He licked his lips, drawing her eye to his mouth and making her want things. "I...guess I am."

Her heart thudded. "Do you think that's smart? People might talk."

He put his arms on her desk and leaned forward. "I have news for you, Becks. They're already talking."

"I know. The Cypress fishbowl." She blew out a breath. "Okay. Why not?"

His smile was bright, and nearly took her breath. People might be talking. She so didn't want to know exactly what they were saying, but at the moment she couldn't think of any reason not to prove them all right.

Chapter 6

By the time they finished dinner, the rain had finally stopped. The air held a chill, and a freshness that would always remind Nate of spring. He'd had to push a little for this date, but walking next to her put ideas in his head. What was that thing they said about spring and a man's thoughts? His mother would probably know, but he wouldn't even mention this to her. Knowing the woman, she would be on phone with wedding planners before the words were completely out of his mouth.

They'd caught the attention of just about every other person at the tavern, and they'd all seemed to know Becky. He'd stopped counting the number of people who stopped by their table to say hello, their brows raised slightly as they obviously wondered just what was going on between them. He would have told them just where they could stick their curiosity, but this was Becky's town. Her life was rooted here as deeply as the reeds that grew at the edge of the lakeshore.

As they headed over to the Institute, he pressed his hand to the small of her back. "You sure weren't kidding about the fishbowl."

"Hashtag Cypress Life," she quipped.

"It doesn't bother you, does it?"

She was quiet for a long minute. "Not really. You?"

He just shrugged. He had no experience with any kind of fishbowl, and he'd had no circle of friends to openly intrude in his love life. His relationship with Laura, their life together, had been very insular, with little outside interference. Until she came across the guy she ultimately slept with, that was. That was a whole lot of interference. Rain delay. Tarps on the field. Game called on the count of infidelity.

They walked around back and Becky began to unlock her bike. Her fingers trembled a little, but her face was tilted away from him.

"This is…" She gathered the coils of her bike lock and faced him. "What is this, Nate?"

His heart thumped, but he recognized that she had a right to ask. He would simply give her honesty right now. Lying, he'd always believed, was way too much trouble. If you told the truth, there was no problem remembering the story later.

"This is two friends, at least I hope we're friends, going out to dinner."

"Friends." Her voice was small. "We were more than that once."

Flashes of memory struck him, of raging teenage hormones and the hottest, sweetest kisses he'd ever tasted.

"Becks, I don't know what this is. I'd hoped to get to know you better, now that we're both older."

The shadow of smile played over her face. "And wiser?"

He shrugged. "I don't know about that. I sure hope so, because I was a dumbass back then."

That widened her smile. "Bugs, you might have been a little bit dense but nobody would have ever called you a dumbass."

"A little dense? Okay, I'll take that."

She brushed the raindrops off of the bike seat and wiped her hands on the front of her pants. "You know, you don't have to drive me home tonight."

"You'll get wet."

She smiled, and he watched as she licked her lips. "What was that you said earlier? I'm not made of sugar?"

"You might not be made of sugar, but you sure looked pretty damn sweet."

He stepped closer and bent his head to her. She smelled of flowers and freshness and Becks. He couldn't resist a second longer, so he covered her mouth with his. She tasted like rain and spring and something even sweeter than sugar. Wrapping his arms around her, he kissed her like he'd wanted to since that first night. Hell, since the first time he'd seen her sitting in the stands at one of his baseball games a hundred years ago.

She made a delicious sound in the back of her throat as she pressed against him. His back grew damp from the water drops on the side of his truck, and the chill helped to rein in his urgency. He pulled back, burying his face in the crook of her neck.

"God, Becks."

"Nate," she whispered, pulling back to look up at him. "And what is this?"

He took a quick look around, seeing nobody from the Institute circling the fishbowl at the moment. "This is us, Becks. I'm sorry, but I couldn't resist."

She continued to stare up at him, her eyes shining and her lips wet. "Then don't."

He felt that flash of heat that he'd managed to keep at

bay before tonight. Before Becks, anyway. He stepped away and all but threw her bike in the back of his truck. In a minute they were tangled in the cab of his truck, making out like no time had passed. He'd missed this. Just letting go and feeling…everything.

She was soft and pliant in his arms, and he lifted her and set her in his lap. Straddling him, she laughed and buried her face against his neck. He could feel every inch of her, and her butt fit his hands perfectly. They were evenly matched in their wants. He was damn sure of that.

His fingers tangled in her hair, loose from its ponytail now. His hands stole up the back of her shirt to stroke her warm, smooth skin. He was so hard he could hardly breathe, and this was from doing little more than kissing her.

"Nate." Her voice was breathy. Sexy. "Oh, Bugs."

He kissed her neck before facing her again. "Do you remember that night, Becks?"

He watched as recognition dawned. They'd made out like their plane was going down all those years ago. All hot and heavy in the backseat of his mother's car. He'd sure as hell never pressed her for more than that back then.

"I do." Her expression was sad. "Then you dropped me

off and didn't speak to me for three weeks."

***

Becky caught his wince at her statement. He knew what she was talking about. That sucked. At the time, she'd been sure he was just clueless. That he hadn't meant to "ghost" her.

He took in a breath, shoving his messy waves back off of his brow. "Becks, I wasn't ready that night."

She boggled. "And I was? I was barely sixteen."

"That's not what I meant."

She crossed her arms, leaning as far away from him as their position allowed. It wasn't much, since the steering wheel was at her back and his big body was at her front.

"Then, please. Educate me."

He stroked her face then, a tender motion that made her eyes prick. The expression in his gaze, regret or remembrance, pulled at her.

"I was off to college at the end of the summer. I knew that if I started something with you, it would be something I couldn't do without."

"You weren't a virgin." She snorted. "I was, but that didn't really matter much to me that night."

She thought his cheeks reddened, but it was hard to see

in the half-light coming from the lamppost nearby.

"I wasn't, true. But it wasn't about sex."

He'd touched her all over that night. He'd made her crave things she wouldn't even understand for a long time to come.

"It wasn't? It sure felt like it."

His smile was sweet and surprisingly. "Becks, you were something else. You made me want more that night."

"You're a big boy, Nate. You were the smartest guy I knew. I think you could have figured out how to take care of that particular problem."

"I knew that if I started up with you, I would never be able to leave."

"Cypress?"

"No." He cupped her cheek and ran his thumb over her lower lip. "You."

Her breath caught. "We weren't serious, Nate." Her voice was just a whisper. "You made no promises."

"I would have, though. But here's the thing. I don't think I could have kept them."

Promises. Yeah, she probably would have been hurt even more if he'd made them.

76

"I'd heard you got engaged at UF."

"I did, but it wasn't the same."

"What wasn't the same?"

"The feelings, Becks." He swallowed audibly. "The need."

She blinked hard. "I had no idea you thought of me that way."

"Yeah, I was good at hiding it."

She really was stunned that he'd wanted her so badly back then. There was one thing she knew right now, though. This conversation needed a serious dose of levity, so she wriggled in his lap. His need was very much evident beneath her.

"You're not so great at hiding it tonight either, Bugs."

He laughed, wrapping his arms around her again. "Do you think we can do this?"

She made a show of considering his words, looking around the interior of the truck cab. "Maybe. But one or both of us will end up with bruises tomorrow."

He shot her a warning look. "I meant…this. Everything."

She swallowed. "You want everything?"

"I don't know, but I sure don't want a one-night thing."

Placing her hands on either side of his face, she dropped a kiss on his nose. "Nate, I'm not a one-night thing. And unless I miss my guess, neither are you."

His gaze held cautious hope, and she couldn't help but wonder just what had happened between him and his fiancée.

"Let me take you home?" he asked.

It was a question, and one she knew the answer to. In the space of one week, heck less than one week, they'd flown back to where they'd been ten years ago. They were both different now, but that didn't mean they couldn't pick up where they'd left off. Hot and bothered and needing each other as badly as they ever had.

"Take me home."

Heat flared in his gorgeous blue eyes and he kissed her again. She managed to climb off of his lap and buckle herself in as he started the truck. He gripped the steering wheel, the cords of muscle in his arms flexing. Was he as apprehensive as she was?

This was a big step. She hadn't been with anyone in almost a year, not since Kent the Slug pulled a fast one on her and dropped her just as quickly. Besides, this was Bugs

Bauer. Her old friend. Her old crush. Her current flame, apparently.

They reached her condo in what felt like the longest time and the shortest. His truck was parked, her bike was stowed, and they were soon in each other's arms again.

He was a busy boy with those skilled hands of his. They were lightly calloused, strong and gentle at the same time. His touch on her back when they'd been in his truck had sent shivers through her. His hands on her breasts? She had no words.

"Oh, Bugs."

He kissed her again. Her throat. Her breasts. "Becks, you're so damn beautiful. Even more than I remember."

He came up on his knees and pulled his shirt up and over his head. She leaned up on her elbows, letting her gaze run over him in the warm glow of the salt lamp on the end table.

She placed a hand on his bare chest, stroking down to where a thin line of hair slipped under his waistband. "You're pretty darn beautiful yourself."

He took in a deep breath, and then returned those sculpted lips of his to her nipples. She could feel herself tightening. Growing so hot under his touch. He slipped a hand down her pants and touched her, making her let out a deep moan.

"Becks." He stroked her, again and again until she was begging him to give her the release her body needed. "That's it, baby. That's it."

He suckled her again, and the added pleasure sent her soaring as high as the oaks near the lake. She might have called his name, she wasn't sure at the moment, but her pulse pounded in her ears as she sank deeper into the couch cushions beneath him.

"Are you okay?" His voice was soft, his brow pressed to hers. "Becks?"

She stretched her arms over her head and sighed. "Bugs, you sure know what you're doing."

His chuckle was low and deep, and when she opened her eyes she read his expression. It was starkly carnal, and in that second she wanted nothing more than to take this tangle into her bedroom. That would be dangerous. She knew that. She'd fallen so hard for him ten years ago, and it had taken a long time to recover. Now? She ran her gaze over him and her mouth watered.

Now, she would indulge herself a little bit and keep her heart safe. She sat up and grabbed her phone, and then thumbed through her playlist to find a song they both knew. One they'd made out to on that long-ago night.

"What are you doing, Becks?"

She tapped on the screen and faced him as the song began to play. It was about apologies. About being too late, but she knew it wasn't.

"That song," he said.

She nodded and reached for him. They might not make love tonight, but she would make sure he was as satisfied as she was. Was it too late? Maybe. At this second, though?

She couldn't have cared less.

Chapter 7

Friday morning Nate was up with the birds. Or maybe the early worms, or something like that. Last night had been mind-blowing, and all he and Becky had done was some heavy petting. Some pretty hot and heavy petting, though. He'd seen her aroused before, when he'd been a little too stupid to really know what he was doing. Seeing her give herself over to pleasure? That was something he suspected he would never forget. Not in another ten years and not in a hundred.

When she'd played that song, one he'd heard often enough over the past decade, and then made him lose control just as well? He couldn't help but also remember that last night. They'd been so close and intimate in that backseat of his mother's car. Becks had offered him more than she'd even known. And a hell of a lot more than he could handle. And he'd run. The churning in his belly told him that he was feeling that urge to run again.

"Man up, Nate," he grumbled as he readied for work.

They weren't kids any more. They were both free to explore what was still between them, weren't they? He knew he wanted to know just what else she could do with those clever hands of hers.

"Nate, honey! Breakfast!"

His mother's voice was a much-needed dousing to his wayward thoughts. He devoured what she'd made, today it was a bagel with cream cheese and grape jelly, and drank his mug of coffee.

"So will we visit Cypress on Saturday?" she asked, her eyes alight.

Nate shook his head. "The Sales Center and the models are closed on the weekend, Mom. I'll try to arrange something for Monday."

"Oh. That would be wonderful, Nate. Thank you."

It was on the tip of his tongue to tell her not to inform Skip or Chip about their upcoming visit, but he would cross that bridge if he came to it. He only had the short ride into Cypress to man up and deal with the woman he couldn't seem to get out of his system. One cup of his mother's coffee sure wouldn't do it.

After parking behind the Institute, he circled around front to Cool Beans. The coffee shop was pretty busy, and the chatter among the other customers nearly drowned out the hiss of the cappuccino machine. The workers manning the counter seemed to have a certain rhythm going, though. By the time he stepped up to the counter, he was sure he should grab something for Becky, too.

"What can I get you?" the red-headed guy in front of him asked.

Nate looked into a face that had a lot in common with his favorite redhead. Recognition dawned and he grinned.

"Tommy Rollins?"

The guy smiled back. "Tom now, but yeah." He tilted his head to the side. "Bugs?"

Nate's lips thinned but he nodded. "Yep. How are you?"

"Great, great. Busy. I work here and at the bakery."

"Keeping busy. That's a famous Rollins trait, right?"

Tom agreed. Nate gave him his order for an americano, and then paused.

"What's your sister's favorite coffee?"

"Joy?" Tom blinked. "Wait, wait. Becky?"

Nate nodded, hoping to avoid adding more water to the fishbowl. When he caught a blond woman staring in his direction from her position at the cappuccino machine, he guessed the jig was up. That, and it seemed like all conversation in the coffee shop had come to a dead standstill.

84

"Yes, Becky," he answered.

Tom shrugged. "Not sure." He turned toward the blond woman. "Hey, Gracie? Do you know what Becky likes?"

Nate winced as the blond laughed lightly.

"I'm beginning to think I just might," she said. "Hi, I'm Grace Potter. Owner of Cool Beans."

"Hi, Grace Potter."

She waved a hand, flicking her long blond ponytail over her shoulder with a toss of her head. "Call me Gracie. Can't seem to shake it." Her eyes sparkled. "Bugs, is it?"

"Nate Bauer, actually. Nice to meet you, Gracie."

Grace smiled. "As for coffee, I don't think you can go wrong with a caramel macchiato." She lifted her chin at Becky's brother. "With almond milk, Tom."

Tom repeated the order to Nate, who paid.

"Anyhow, it's great seeing you Nate," Tom said.

"You, too."

Nate felt eyes on him as he stepped aside to wait for his drink. At least talk resumed in the rest of the place. When the blond placed the to-go cups on the counter in front of him, she crossed her arms. "Tell Becky I said 'hi,' will you?"

"Sure."

Keeping his gaze straight ahead, he left the coffee shop. Lettie Fairfax was seated beneath a crepe myrtle in what he guessed was her favorite table she'd spoken of yesterday.

"Good morning, Nate Bauer," she called.

"Good morning, ma'am."

"And do tell our dear girl good morning for me?"

Nate started to make some sort of objection, but in the end he simply nodded. Tom and Grace and Lettie all seemed to know about him and Becky, so who was he to put up a fight?

When he arrived at the Institute, Becky was just rushing toward her desk. She skidded to a stop when she saw him, and then a gorgeous smile spread across her face.

"Good morning, Bugs."

Nate grinned and held the coffee cups aloft. "Good morning, Becks."

Her eyes rounded. "Tell me one of those is for me."

"Caramel Macchiato, on the advice of Grace Potter."

Becky made a happy little sound before stashing her bike helmet under her desk. Her hair was wild this morning, loose again, as she took the cup from him. Bringing it to her nose, she breathed in and sighed. "Gracie sure knows her stuff."

Nate took the lid off of his coffee and had to agree. The brew smelled fantastic. "Saw your little brother, too."

"Not so little now, right? He got the height genes from our dad and Joy and I got the leftovers."

He ran his gaze over Becky, cute and fresh-looking in her shorts and polo. "I don't know about your sister but your just about right, as far as I can tell."

Her cheeks bloomed pink and she shook her head. "Watch it, Bugs. People will start to talk."

He leaned his arms on her desk. "Becks, you and I know they're already talking. Hell, they've probably been talking since last Monday."

***

Her brow furrowed. He was right, of course. It was inevitable. "Yeah, sorry about that."

"I can handle it if you can." His eyes got all dreamy and she wrapped both hands around her coffee cup to keep from touching him. "Can you?"

There was weight to what he was asking. He knew it. She knew it. After last night, though? When he'd made her feel all sorts of things and whispered such sweet and naughty words? How could she not?

"I think it's worth a shot, Bugs."

To her surprise his expression grew tender. "I think it's worth more than a shot. But I'll take that for now."

He touched her hand and then walked down the hallway toward his office. Slumping down into her seat, she sipped at her perfectly-made coffee. Tom would pepper her with questions when she saw him next. Not to mention the grilling Grace would put her through if and when they ever managed to have a girls' night out in the foreseeable future.

Friday at the Cypress Institute could be as busy as a Monday, given it was closed on the weekend like the Sales Center. Ty had back-to-back tours, which Becky coordinated. The director had a few meetings as well, with the builder and architect of the Active Adult community. There was talk of expanding it even before the first twenty homes were occupied. All of that boded well for Cypress Corners, in Becky's considered opinion.

Lunch was a quick run to the market for a ready-made sandwich before diving into the coming week's schedule. She saw Nate's name pop up several times, but it didn't cause the awkwardness it had just a few days earlier. No. Now she had lovely little shivers to go with the memories of last night. Sadly, that was all she saw of him throughout the entire day.

As the afternoon wore on, she steadily and methodically clicked through all she had to do. By the time five o'clock rolled around, she was eager to start her weekend. She wasn't quite sure of all that would entail, but she sure hoped she'd see more of Bugs.

"Hey, there," Harmony said.

"Hey."

"So you're coming on Sunday?"

Becky nodded. "My mother's nose will be out of joint, since she likes to do a family dinner on Sundays. But at least I won't—" She stopped herself, but Harmony caught her.

"At least you won't what?"

She blew out a breath. "I won't have to face the inquisition."

"About a certain guy we're all just getting to know?"

Becky nodded. "Tom was working at Cool Beans this morning."

"And Nate brought you a cup of coffee."

The empty cup still sat on Becky's desk. "Yep."

"But that's sweet."

89

"Yes, it is. And Tom will want to know why."

Harmony's mouth curved in a sly smile Becky seldom saw on her face. "I seem to remember your brother spiking Kent's favorite drink with salt for a while last year."

"And I don't even know how Tom knew about that slug."

"No?" Harmony placed her hands on her hips. "Just who do you think sits under that crepe myrtle all day long, hmm?"

"Of course it has to be Lettie. And I can't fault my little brother."

"He loves you."

Becky knew that. And she loved Joy and Tom right back. "We're a loyal bunch, we Rollins."

"That's what I heard." Her eyes brightened. "So will you bring Nate with you on Sunday?"

"Nate's a big boy, Harmony. I'm sure he can manage to bring himself."

"Bring myself where?" Nate asked as he joined them.

"To our house, Nate," Harmony said. "The barbecue, remember?"

"I do. Looking forward to it."

Harmony beamed at him and winked in Becky's direction. "See you both there, then."

She left them and Becky held up her hands. "Sorry, Nate."

"Just so you know, Becks. Anywhere you want to bring me, I'll go willingly."

Heat flashed over her and she bit her lip. "Good to know."

He gave her a long look that caused more of those tingles, and then she was alone at her desk again. That was a good thing since, after that exchange, she sure needed a little time to herself to recover. Thank goodness she didn't live at the inn anymore.

"Hi, sis!"

Her sister Joy bounced over to her desk not much later, a big smile on her face. Becky stood and wrapped her in a hug. "What's up?"

"Zach wants to head to the End Zone tonight."

Becky pulled back, tilting her head to the side. "And?"

"And he's tired of losing to me."

"Can't Chase shoot a game of pool tonight?"

Joy nodded. "He can, but Zach wanted me to ask Nate

to come too."

"What does that have to do with me exactly?"

Joy leveled a know-it-all look their mother had perfected years ago and Becky rolled her eyes.

"Will you ask him?" Joy asked. "Wings and pool, sis. Nothing better." She laughed. "Well, I can think of a few things."

Becky put her sister's slightly racy comment out of her head as she picked up her phone and sent Nate a message. He got right back to her and, just like that, she had a date on a Friday night for the first time in ages.

"There." Becky placed her phone down on the desk once more. "Happy?"

Joy studied her for a long minute, her eyes narrowed. "Yes, but I bet I'm not the only one."

Becky tried to wave that away but she couldn't ignore the bubble of excitement. She was going out with Nate again.

Her inner teenager squealed with delight and she couldn't hide her smile.

Chapter 8

Nate parked his truck in the lot at the End Zone, a popular sports bar in St. Cloud. The spaces were nearly filled, mostly with other pickups and motorcycles. It was a Friday night, but he hadn't been there much in the past to judge whether or not this was usual. Laura hadn't liked the place and, truth be told, he hadn't been much for crowds back then. He liked to take in games there though, since Laura hadn't liked sports much, either.

In the two years since their breakup, he was finally beginning to see what he should have recognized before. They really hadn't been a very good match. She'd been comfortable. Serene and calm, and their relationship had been just as steady. Steady and dull, he realized as he recalled just how unsteady even just being around Becky Rollins made him feel. Hell, breathing in her wildflower scent was enough to spike his heartrate. With her sitting with him in his truck right now, he had ample evidence to that.

He'd been both surprised and psyched when Becky had invited him tonight, and hadn't even hesitated before giving her his answer. He might be clueless when it came to…whatever this was, but he wasn't going to miss the chance to spend more time with her.

"Looks crowded tonight," Becky said.

He glanced at her, unable to keep from running his gaze all over her. She'd gone home to change after work, and casual date-night Becks was a lot to take. A soft-looking blue Henley tucked into jeans. Little half-boots or whatever they called them on her feet. And her hair. It was loose again, and a mess of waves he longed to touch.

"Do you think your sister's already here?"

"She texted me that she and Zach will have already staked out a table. No grass grows under Joy's feet."

"Or yours, if I remember correctly."

She shrugged. "We don't tend to do patience very well."

"Yeah." He couldn't help but recall just how eager she'd been last night. "I saw that."

She gaped at him, and then laughed. "Quit teasing me, Bugs."

"Hey, I'm not making any promises."

He got out and walked around to her side. She actually let him open her door, which said she could show a little bit of patience, and they went into the sports bar.

The interior was dim but the large dining room to the

94

right was lined all around with bright TV screens set high on the walls broadcasting fishing shows and Ultimate Fighting matches. Surprisingly an emo nineties song played from the digital jukebox but the scent of French fries and buffalo wings hung tantalizingly in the air.

There were only a few families seated at the wooden tables and booths, but plenty of couples and pairs of couples. Friday night was date night, apparently. There did look to be single guys and girls hugging the long bar at the back of the cavernous space too, so he guessed this was probably a pretty good place to meet somebody.

Nate urged Becky ahead of him as they made their way toward a booth set against one wall. He could see her sister waving as they approached.

"You made it," Joy said as she hugged her sister. "The place is packed."

Becky nodded. "Haven't been here on a Friday in a while."

Joy made the introductions. Nate nodded to Zach and shook hands with his brother Chase, who looked a lot like Zach.

"Cypress baseball, right?" Chase asked him.

95

"Yep. Did you play?"

Chase shook his head. "Nope. That was Zach's thing." He introduced Nate to his wife, a pretty woman with light red hair. "This is my wife, Carrie."

"Nice to meet you, Carrie."

There was some jostling, but the big booth could accommodate even three guys their size along with Joy, Carrie and Becky. The seating arrangement was agreeable to Nate, though. He was right next to Becky, and he wouldn't trade that spot for anything.

They talked about the stables, Zach's brainchild, being built out on the east side of Cypress. When Chase talked about the farm and petting zoo run by Billy Harris, Nate's ears pricked up.

"Is that run by another brother?" he asked.

"No, Billy is our cousin," Zach answered. "Like a brother now, though."

Chase nodded his agreement. Nate envied the Harris men. He'd been raised alone, by a mother who could be emotionally needy at times. He'd had baseball, though. His teammates in school had made up for that solitude. Not for the first time, he wondered what would have happened if he'd played in college. Not that there had been much time for ball. Aside from his studies, he'd had nothing but the occasional night out until he'd met Laura.

"We ordered a platter of wings," Chase said.

"The big platter," his wife added with a laugh.

A server came by, a beefy dark-haired guy with a goatee. "Wings are on the way. What's everybody drinking?"

The brothers shared a shrug and said, "How about a pitcher?" at the same time.

Joy shook her head. "That happens all the time."

"A pitcher sounds good," Nate said.

"Six glasses," Joy and Becky said in unison, and the rest of them chuckled.

Nate was quiet, but he sensed a comfort with this group that he hadn't expected. True, he'd known Zach a little bit in high school. And he'd gone to school with both the Rollins girls. Tonight had a distinct couple vibe, and he wasn't yet sure how he felt about that. Two years was a long time to go without having a partner other than occasional hookups. This thing with Becky? It felt like nothing he'd ever had. Before or after his engagement.

The wings were pretty great and the beer was cold and

sudsy. The women ordered nachos, Becky insisted that they needed the vegetables as she ate the chopped tomatoes off the top of her chips, and the rest of them talked and laughed.

When the time came to rack up the balls, he was feeling like he wouldn't mind hanging out with this particular group of people again. The enjoyment on Becky's beautiful face was clear and her laugh? It was his second favorite sound she made, right after those sweet moans he'd heard last night.

They made their way to a huge room to the right of the bar. He saw there were six pool tables in there, along with several retro arcade and pinball machines. Dartboards took up one wall to the back, and guys were jostling for position and trash-talking to impress their dates.

"Bugs, you look surprised," Becky said. "Haven't you been here before?"

"Not in a long time and not very often."

"But you were a jock."

"Back when I was too young to legally drink, Becks."

She nudged him with her shoulder. "True." She rubbed her hands together. "Now, teams? Girls against guys?"

Carrie held up her hands, backing away from the table. "Sure, but don't expect me to contribute anything of value to the team."

From the dining area he caught a bit of the song now playing on the jukebox. It was that song. From long ago. From just last night. Grabbing Becky's hand, he tugged her closer.

"Win or lose, it's not too late."

Her brow furrowed, and then smoothed as she obviously picked up enough of the song to get his meaning. "We'll see, Bugs. We'll see."

***

"That was fun," Nate said as they drove back toward Cypress.

"You almost sound surprised."

"I am, a little. These are your people, Becks. But they didn't make me feel like the odd man out."

"You're not odd." She laughed. "Quirky, maybe."

He eyed her, shaking his head before facing forward again. "Thanks for coming out with me."

She nodded, staring out her window as the streetlights disappeared. They were nearly back at Cypress, and this long stretch of road between St. Cloud and home was unlit and underpopulated. They didn't speak much on the ride, but

Becky knew that gifted mind of his was working furiously. She could tell by the little ridge evident between his brows.

He parked in her driveway and switched off the engine. "Thanks again," he said, turning in his seat to face her.

"Nate, you don't have to keep thanking me. You're nobody's charity case."

He smiled, and the expression was sweet and a little sad. "Yeah, but when I think about what we could have had back then if I hadn't been such a pussy? I could kick myself."

"We were both young." She reached out and touched his hand. "Besides, it's not too late to make up for lost time."

Heat flared in his eyes and, just like that, she knew he was going to come up to her place tonight. He kissed her, hard, and they both were breathing a little fast as they entered the condo.

"Do you want some coffee?" she asked, kissing his throat. "Soda?"

"No, I'm good." He kissed her ear, and then tugged on the lobe with his teeth. "I have everything I need right here."

His hands were on her butt, so she figured she'd take his word on that. Her hands were up around his neck and tangled in his thick hair, so she was pretty happy with what was right in front of her too.

He soon had her under him on her nice comfy Ikea couch, driving her crazy with that beautiful mouth of his. His kisses were hot. Hungry. His lips and tongue were insistent as they traveled down her body toward the place that needed him so desperately right now.

"Nate, please," she gasped.

"Easy, Becks." He kissed the inside of her thigh as his fingers stroked her. His touch was slow and steady, like him. "Let's make this last."

"Bugs, don't make me beg!"

He laughed, low and soft, and gave in to her pleas. He was clearly as skilled with his tongue as he was with his hands, and she was soon sobbing his name as her climax took her.

When she opened her eyes she found him gazing at her with an expression that, if she had to guess, was a combination of masculine pride and desperate need.

"Becks, you're as sweet as you look."

She sucked in a breath. His words were simple and so hot she nearly swooned. She managed to come up on her knees, and then took his face in her hands.

"Turnabout is fair play, isn't it?"

He nodded. "I think it just might be."

Pushing at his chest with all of her strength, she switched positions with him. His shirt was gone, she didn't remember taking it off earlier but she couldn't remember much about what had happened once he put those big hands on her, so she kissed him all over. Flicking one of his nipples with her tongue, she relished the moan of surrender that came from him.

As she stroked him like she had last night, she felt the strength in him. His pants were easy to loosen, and he was soon in her hands. Without another second to waste, she took him in her mouth.

"God, Becks!"

He arched toward her and she began to drive him as crazy as he had her. Sucking and licking him, she gave in to every fantasy she'd ever had of him. Once she'd been old enough to realize just what they might have shared, that was. Tonight she would send him over the edge.

His response fueled her enthusiasm, and she moaned herself as his heart pounded beneath her hand splayed in the middle of his chest. His groans grew louder, and she was grateful that the construction of her condo was as solid as any of the houses built in Cypress. He could moan to his heart's content and none of her neighbors would be any the wiser. At least, she hoped so.

As he pumped his hips beneath her hold, close to his climax, she took all of him again. He caved, moaning her name as he came.

Feeling pretty darn proud of herself, she draped her body over his and kissed his open mouth. His arms came up around her, holding her tight as he apparently caught his breath.

"Damn, Becks."

She kissed his chin, and then his chest. "If you thank me again, I'll deck you."

His laugh was deep now, and shook them both. "Okay, I give."

Chapter 9

When Nate finally rolled out of bed around eleven on Saturday morning, he was thinking he could get used to having Becky in his arms. He sure missed her this morning. She'd seemed just as happy to keep him at her place last night, and he'd stayed there until the early hours. He'd been afraid to push for more, although after what they'd shared he was pretty sure "more" would probably kill him in the best way, so he'd left the weekend open-ended.

He made his way to the kitchen, where he found his mother had made what he knew she called a big country breakfast. They had a visitor, too. Skip or Chip, and the guy was drinking coffee out of Nate's "Quit bugging me" mug.

"Good morning, honey!" his mother sang.

"Good morning." He eyed her latest crush. "Hello."

"Nate honey, this is Chip," his mother said. "Chip, this is my son Nate."

"Hello, son. Good to meet you."

Nate ground his teeth. He might not have any idea who his father was, but he was as sure as hell it wasn't this shiny guy. He looked to be around sixty, and obviously took good care of himself. He was deeply tan, probably from playing golf or tennis. His hair was salt-and-pepper, and thick. He also had way too many teeth, in Nate's opinion.

Nate nodded and pulled out a chair. "What brings you by, Skip?"

"Chip." The man laughed lightly. "Your mother invited me for breakfast last night."

Alarm flashed through Nate. "What?"

His mother giggled and held up her hands. "Not that way, honey! Chip and I met up, quite by accident, when the girls and I went to the buffet."

Chip's ruddy cheeks turned ruddier under Nate's scrutiny. *By accident, my ass.*

"When your mother invited me to break my fast with the two of you, I couldn't refuse."

Nate grunted in answer to that pompous statement. "What are you up to today, Mom?"

She pouted and sat down beside him. "I'd hoped to go out to Cypress Corners with you today, but after you told me that all of the models are closed on the weekends I was at a loss."

"So I thought I would take your mother for a drive out to the water," Chip said. "Maybe grab lunch on the

105

Intercoastal."

Nate was torn. While it might be nice to have a Saturday to himself for once, he didn't trust this *Cosmopepla conspicillaris*. The guy was as showy as the hedgenettle stink bug, and just about as welcome.

The hope shining on his mother's face was hard to ignore, though. And it would give him a chance to head over to Cypress on his own if she were otherwise occupied.

"That sounds nice," Nate said to her. "Have a good time."

Her eyes lit up, and he acknowledged to himself just how much she depended on him. What if he had told her no? Would she have bowed to his demand?

When the hell had he become the parent? Damn, he had to get his own place sooner rather than later. He couldn't stand to wait to start his own life until she moved into the Active Adult community.

After downing a few pancakes and a couple of eggs, he excused himself and returned to his room. Withdrawing his laptop, he settled on the bed and began to search. The Sales Center might be closed on the weekends but that didn't mean he had to wait until Monday to see if there was anything available to rent himself.

He soon found a two-bedroom, and sent an inquiry. To his surprise, the condo unit offered for sublet wasn't far from the town square. He made arrangements for that afternoon to see it, and then sent Becky a text.

Morning, Becks.

A couple of seconds later she replied.

Hey there, Bugs. What's up?

He thought for a minute. *Lunch today?*

She seemed to think for a little bit longer than he had before answering. *Sure. Where?*

You pick. I'm up for anything.

Apparently.

He could practically hear her laughter from fifteen miles away. *I'll let you know when I'm in Cypress.*

Cool.

He set his phone down. Just like that, he had another date. Maybe this relationship stuff wasn't so difficult after all?

"And maybe this is just a date, dumbass," he said to himself.

His mother and the stink bug were gone by the time

he'd showered and dressed. The weather was finally turning warmer, although finally was relatively early as far as Central Florida went, so he chose cargo shorts and a navy blue polo. A pair of his favorite boat shoes and he was ready for wherever Becky decided she wanted to eat.

The drive to Cypress Corners wasn't a long one, but he was really looking forward to the time when he wouldn't have to make the commute. Working there, and dating there, put a big chunk of his life in the pretty community. If things went south with Becky, although it was early days to think along those lines, his life could get complicated. That possibility was always there, ever since he'd started working at the Institute. Living in Cypress wouldn't make things any more difficult. He wasn't going to go borrowing trouble, though. He'd just take things as they came, and leave the worrying for now.

He pulled his truck up to the curb in front of her building and looked at the number. It seemed familiar somehow, so he drew out his phone and checked the notes on the available sublet. Yep. It was a unit in her building.

"Of course it is," he mumbled.

"Of course what is, Bugs?" Becky asked, bouncing

down from the front porch.

He slipped his phone back into his pocket and shrugged. "We just might be neighbors, Becks."

***

Becky blinked, and then nodded sagely as it hit her. Mrs. Barnes was moving to Boca Raton and planned to lease her place.

"The sublet across the hall from my condo?" she asked. "Are you moving in?"

He stuck his hands in the front pockets of his cargo shorts, tugging them down a bit to show his flat and fit lower belly. "I'm not sure, but I have an appointment to see it this afternoon."

"Yes, she said she wanted to move to Boca and soon."

"Would it bother you, Becks?" He brushed his hair back and gave her a small smile. "If I moved in next door?"

Would it? She thought for a minute. It would be very convenient to have him an arm's length away, but it could get messy. Still, she wasn't ever going to be the girl who dictated what everyone in her orbit should do, let alone the guy she was seeing.

"It wouldn't bother me," she told him. "You?"

109

He stepped closer, touching her cheek as if he couldn't stand to wait another second. "Not in the least."

He kissed her, and she forgot about any awkwardness or anything else that might happen if they shared such close quarters. They were out in front of her building right now, kissing in the sunshine as though it was the most natural thing in the world. If she knew her neighbors, especially the sweet and nosy Mrs. Barnes, everybody would soon know of her involvement with their building's newest tenant.

Catching her breath, she rested her brow on his chest. "People will talk, Bugs. Again."

"Let them." He lifted her chin and kissed her again, then stepped back. "Now, where do you want to go for lunch?"

"Have you been to the Boathouse?"

"Cold beer and gator tail? Yeah, I've been there. Not in a while, though."

She clicked her tongue. "That is a real shame."

"Do you want to take one of the boats over there?"

Pleased to her toes, she nodded. "Let's."

They got into his truck and headed for the main lakeshore. It was a Saturday, and it seemed like the place was packed. It was a beautiful morning, so that was no surprise.

Kids were happily scrambling all over the play structures and the swings were squeaking and creaking. The sounds combined to make a pleasant racket, and as she and Nate got out of his truck she recognized a few familiar faces. Ty and Cassie Walsh were chasing his niece and Ben and Tammy Chapman were pushing their dark-haired little girl in one of the swings.

"Seems like the place to be," he said.

"Welcome to Cypress on the weekends, Bugs." She craned her neck to get a better view of the dock. "Looks like a few boats are free."

She waved to her friends as she and Nate made their way over to the dock. She could read the curiosity on both Tammy and Cassie's faces but just lifted her chin and ignored them. They would think what they wanted and, since she and Nate were seeing each other, she wasn't going to deny anything at this point.

The boats available in Cypress were either wind or electric powered, which kept the noise at a minimum and the risk of pollution low. It looked like there were two sailboats and an electric pontoon boat available, along with a sleek-looking skiff powered by solar panels adorning the roof.

"Ride the sun today, Becks?" Nate asked her.

It was a cozy ride, with two curved bench seats facing each other. The motor was manageable, but she doubted she would have to pilot it today.

"Sounds good to me," she answered.

Nate signed out the boat and they boarded. On the north side of the lake, the waterway narrowed to an inlet as it fed into a larger lake. This one boasted both gas and electric powered boats and jet skis, and was very busy today.

"Lots of traffic," Nate observed.

"I prefer our lake, thanks. Maybe we can't zoom around but it's so much more quiet."

"Let chance of pollution on our lake, too."

She caught his note of possessiveness and grinned. "Our lake, huh? Feeling like Cypress is getting a hold of you?"

"Part of Cypress, Becks." His eyes sparkled. "For sure."

She flushed and dipped her head as they neared the dock behind the Boathouse. It was nearly full, but Nate ably steered their little boat into an available slip. He jumped out and secured the line, appearing very sure.

"Do you sail, Nate?"

"Some. Kayak more, though."

"I've done that, too."

He straightened. "We'll have to go together sometime. Before it gets too hot, anyway."

"So, like, in two days."

He laughed with her and gave her his hand. "Careful."

Her hand in his felt very right, and she couldn't resist giving it a little squeeze before letting go. He waved her ahead of him and they walked over the sun-warmed boards to the restaurant.

The place was the definition of rustic, and looked like something out of an old painting. Muted colors, faded boards and a rusted tin roof. It had atmosphere up the yin-yang, and she loved its Old Florida feel.

The Boathouse was loud and crowded and filled with wooden picnic tables. It felt like it could be any place in the country, frequented by locals and never drawing many tourists. The hostess showed them to a scarred picnic table near the wide screened windows and she sat on the bench across from Nate.

It felt like they were still outside. The chirps and croaks of everything that was coming to life at this time of year were loud through the windows. The air was pretty comfortable, moved by ceiling fans above. Sunlight filtered through the screened windows, and she thought that she couldn't imagine a more perfect setting for lunch with Bugs Bauer.

A server, an older woman whom Becky recognized, came over with a smile. "Becky Rollins. Look what the cat dragged in."

Becky shook her head. "Hello, Betsy. No cat."

"No, no cat." Betsy narrowed her eyes on Nate as she pushed her blond hair back from her brow. "Who's your friend?"

"Nate Bauer, ma'am," Nate answered.

"Bauer? Are you Donna's boy?"

"I am."

Betsy waved a hand. "Thought as much. You have the look of her." She smiled. "Now, what can I get you two for lunch?"

Chapter 10

Saturday afternoon, after sharing a great lunch and a
nice if warm boat ride back to the main lakeshore, Nate was
rethinking the wisdom of moving into Becky's building.
While he really liked hanging out with her, and doing a lot
more than hanging out with her, he knew things could get
messy. She might have brushed off that possibility, but he
knew better himself. He was no good at complications.
Uncomplicated was the best thing he could say about his past
relationship with Laura, after all. That sure was the truth.

As he stepped out of the available unit, with a loaf of
zucchini bread from the lovely Mrs. Barnes, he knew there
wasn't any going back. The terms were ideal, a three-month
sublease with the option to buy the condo if she decided to
sell. It would be close quarters, living there with his mother,
but they were going to look at quick move-in houses on
Monday. Hopefully he'd be living alone soon. And anything
he got up to with his gorgeous neighbor would be his
business.

He'd dropped Becky back home before meeting with
Mrs. Barnes, and now figured he would kill an hour or so
driving around Cypress. He couldn't shake the feeling that

this would change things with Becks, but he was determined to figure out what they could be to each other now. So he and the zucchini bread took a ride.

He knew that Cypress was made up of several villages, some expansive and some more densely-populated. From what he could see, homes large and small catered to families of all sizes and finances, though they all seemed to be constructed as well as the very building he was considering making his new home.

Classically designed, in styles like craftsman, colonial and traditional, the houses were also state-of-the-art at their guts. Wired for convenience and technology, not to mention an eye toward conservation and green sensibilities, Cypress appeared to be a great place to settle. It sure seemed that he was doing just that now.

He might only be twenty-eight but he sure as hell wasn't getting any younger. He'd once thought he'd be married by now, and nearly had been. Hell, he'd even thought he'd have a child by now too. At least there hadn't been one from his failed engagement. Raising a child without the kind of affection he'd seen so clearly among those families at the lakeshore would have really screwed up a little kid.

116

His mother might have raised Nate with lots of affection, but there was still a part of him that wondered just who his father was. He'd long since given up asking his mother. He used to all the time, when he was a kid.

Playing little league and seeing all of those dads in the stands, knowing not one of them was his, had sucked big time. One night he'd screwed up his courage and peppered her with questions until she'd burst into tears. Her emotions always seemed very close to the surface, and he learned early on that he would much rather cause smiles and laughter than those big, wet tears.

Shaking off those memories, he parked the truck at the curb and stepped out. The sights and sounds of the crowded lakeshore hit him in the face, and it was very homey. It wasn't what he was used to, but by the laughter he could hear and the fun he could almost feel, he figured it was a damn good way to spend a Saturday. Aside from his earlier boat ride with Becky.

"Hey, Nate!"

Nate looked up to see Harmony Chapman waving at him from a spot next to the playground structure. She was up on her toes, and wearing a big smile. Though it was probably going to lead to trouble, Nate walked on over to her.

"Hi, Harmony. What's up?"

"Just doublechecking that you and Becky will be at the barbecue tomorrow." She tilted her head, her eyes bright. "You will be bringing Becky, won't you?"

Nate waited a beat to get his answer just right. How would Becks feel if he said yes? Or if he said he wasn't sure?

"I'm coming, Harmony. I believe Becky is coming, too."

She seemed to be expecting more from him, but he wasn't going to give it to her. If Becky wanted to declare that they were together, that was totally her call. When Harmony gave a short nod, he knew she'd gotten the message. He also had the impression that he'd passed some sort of test, but he had no clue what it was.

"Can I bring anything?" he asked.

Her brows arched, and she smiled. "Just bring what you'd like to drink, I think. Becky likes Moscato. Just sayin'."

He let that slide and just nodded. "Will do."

A little boy with dark hair came running over to her and grabbed her hand. "Come on, Mom! Dad wants to head over to Uncle Jake's place."

"The Adventure Trails," Harmony said to Nate in explanation. "Time to climb a wall, I guess."

The two of them waved and then walked off toward the path that led around the lake to the Adventure Trails. Nate knew there was kids' section there too, but considered running the big trails tomorrow. Like a local.

He'd made a decision about his new living arrangements, and had to tell his mother. Then, on Monday, they were going to try to find a place for her too. It all seemed to be happening pretty damn fast, but for once in his life he was going to pull out all the stops.

No more keeping things smooth and uncomplicated. Life was messy, and it was about time he got his hands dirty. Inevitably, his mind went to Becky and what they'd shared so far. It hadn't even been two weeks since they got reacquainted, but it felt like the most natural thing in the world. He wouldn't let his past, his behavior or his experiences, get in his way now. He wanted to live his own damn life. His own damn way.

To that end, he got back into his truck and left Cypress, bound for the house he would only share with his mother for a little more time.

***

"We're going to look at the Active Adult section on Monday," Nate told her.

They were waiting for a pizza at her place, and Becky could admit to herself that hanging out with him was pretty nice. She did love her apartment, decorated with stuff from Ikea and flea market finds. The couch was a sleek gray thing, but the fat pillows on it were done in faded pastels. She had a shabby-chic thing going, and liked it. Nate looked pretty good on that couch. Just like last night when they'd gotten all tangled up in each other.

She poured herself a glass of the chilled Moscato he'd brought and handed him a beer from the six-pack she'd bought for him. "She must be excited."

"It's her default setting most days, but yeah."

His words might sound derisive, but they clearly weren't when taken with the fondness in his tone and the affection in his gaze.

Settling on the couch beside him, she tucked her feet beneath her. They hadn't talked about his new living situation, and she was a little hesitant to bring it up. "And am

I to assume she'll be living with you in Mrs. Barnes' place?"

The corners of his eyes crinkled as he laughed lightly. "Not if I can help it."

"Nate!"

He held up his hands. "Becks, she's been living with me for almost two years now."

She bit her lower lip as she mulled that over. "Since your breakup?"

He nodded. "I didn't want to stay in the apartment I shared with Laura, so I found a new place. As luck would have it, my mom's latest had decided to go back to his wife around the same time."

She winced. "Ouch."

He took a long drink of his beer and shook his head. "Yeah. She was convinced he was the one."

"That seems to be a common thread with her."

"It is. I'm hoping that, with the move to Cypress, both of us can leave all that baggage behind."

"You know, baggage has a way of following you."

He arched a brow. "I think I saw that on a T-shirt."

She pushed at his shoulder and laughed. "I'm just saying that, even as young and vital as we both most certainly are, there are things in our pasts that never really go away."

"Are you speaking personally, or in general?"

"Personally." She set her wineglass on the coffee table and sighed. "I made a big mistake last year. Dated a real slug man who wasn't quite as divorced as he'd led me to believe."

"Slug man?"

"Slimy, through and through." She laughed a little. "Actually, my little brother spiked his drinks at the coffee shop with salt for a while afterwards."

"Salt for a slug?" He nodded. "That would do it."

"And are *you* speaking personally or in your capacity as the bug man of Cypress Corners?"

"Bug Man. Hmm. Better than Slug Man, I guess."

A flush spread over her as she realized just how much better he was than Kent could ever hope to be. Bugs was a better man. One who worked hard, was respected and loved his mother. Better for her, to be sure. Her heart began to race, and it had as much to do with her physical reaction to Nate as to the fact that she seemed to be racing toward getting way too involved way too fast.

Thankfully, the doorbell rang. Popping up out of her seat, she crossed to the door and pulled it open. She grabbed the pizza from the kid in the hallway. "I tipped on the card," she told him.

He nodded and she closed the door. When she turned back around, Nate was staring at her with those pretty blue eyes. He seemed to be mulling something over his that gifted brain of his.

"Okay, Bugs." She set the pizza on the tall counter separating her kitchenette from the living space. "Spill."

He straightened and walked over to her, closing his hands over the back of one of her two stools set near the counter. "Spill what?"

"I can see that you're thinking, Nate. Your mind is going through circles, and it can't only be because you caught the scent of meat and cheese."

He shrugged and thumbed open the pizza box. "I do like meat and cheese, but I've been thinking about something else."

Her heart did that flutter thing again and she discreetly braced her hands on the edge of the counter. "Do I want to know?"

"I'm not sure." Letting the lid drop on the box, he faced her fully. "Becks, this is going somewhere. I feel it."

She swallowed and gave a nod. "I do, too."

Relief was clear on his face as he rolled his eyes. "Thank God."

That made her laugh, and then she sobered when she saw that his brows were drawn together. "You're not just talking about the naughty stuff, are you?"

In a blink of an eye he cupped her face with his big hands, his eyes deep. "Becks, this isn't just about the naughty stuff."

He kissed her, giving her more of that deliciousness that affected her like no other man's ever had. When he broke contact, he brushed a light kiss over her forehead. Taking in a bracing breath, she brushed his hair back and smiled.

"Let's eat this meat and cheese, then." She patted his cheek and circled around the counter to the other side. "I think we're going to need the protein."

Heat flared in Nate's eyes and they ate their dinner. In a heartbeat afterwards they were back on the couch, wrapped tightly in each other. His kisses tasted like garlic and beer, and yet spicy somehow. His scent, always fresh and heady, filled her senses.

"I couldn't wait to touch you again," he said, nuzzling

her throat. "Ah, Becks."

He was tickling her, and it was funny and hot. "I've seen my little brother inhale his food, but I think you beat his record tonight."

Lifting his head, he grinned down at her. "I had great incentive."

She slipped out from under him and took his hand in hers. "Let's go to my bedroom."

He stood and followed where she led, stopping halfway there to tug her close and kiss her again. Her belly fluttered and her body heated as she came in full contact with him. They made their way into her bedroom and pulled at each other's clothes as they fell onto the bed. When they were both nearly naked, he lifted his head and looked around, his brows arched.

"This room is the mirror image of the one in my apartment," he said.

She followed his gaze, to the wide windows set to left side and the opened closet door on the right. Her bathroom, big for a one-bedroom place in her opinion, was set just beyond the closet.

"Your apartment?" She came up on her elbows. "You're

taking it, then?"

He nodded and came in for another kiss. "I am. The bathroom's on the other side."

"This is an odd conversation to be having half naked, Nate. Are you saying this is opposite day?"

"Huh?"

She sat up and wrapped her arms around him. "Just asking if you want me to be on top."

He blinked, and then gave her a slow shake of his head. "Nope." He stretched out again, pushing her flat against the memory foam mattress. "I like you just where you are, Becks."

He began to use those clever hands on her and she closed her eyes. "Me, too."

Chapter 11

Nate hadn't lied. Having Becky spread beneath him, his face buried in her hair and her arms wrapped around his neck, was just about as perfect as things could get. His dumb statement about the bedroom had just slipped out earlier, but he was going to live right across the hall from her. That was a fact. Shutting his mind off and just feeling was never something he was good at doing. Tonight he'd focus on Becks and how friggin' fantastic she felt beneath him.

Using his hands, he wrung sighs and gasps out of her as he ramped up the pleasure. He'd kept on his boxer briefs, but that thin layer of cotton was hardly any barrier. Her sweet heat, the narrow strip of silky hair between her thighs, rubbed him just the right way.

"Oh, Nate." Her voice was weak and needy, and very arousing. "Yes."

He kissed her mouth again, his tongue delving inside to taste more of her, and then moved to tease and savor her gorgeous breasts. Lifting his head, he took a hot second to run his gaze over her. Her skin was flushed, her eyes dark and dreamy, and he gave a silent prayer that this was finally happening. He was going to finally have his Becks.

"Are you sure, Becks?" he asked, so damn worried she would say no that he nearly lost his breath.

She bit that full lower lip, swollen now from his frantic kisses, and nodded. "Oh, yeah."

He let out a whoop, he couldn't seem to help it, and grabbed his pants off of the floor. He'd tucked in a couple of condoms and boy was he happy about that right now.

Taking care of it, with shaking hands no less, he was soon right there. So close to making her his. He hesitated for a beat, and then sank inside of her. She was hot and tight, and fit him perfectly. Closing his eyes, he began to move.

Becky held on to him tightly, bowing back as she took all of him. They moved in rhythm, climbing higher toward climax. Fast. Faster than he might have hoped for, because his own pleasure was coming on him hard. Becky came first, crying out his name as he continued to move with her. Mentally reciting the names of all of the breeds of spiders indigenous to Central Florida, he fought to hold on to his control.

"Nate!" She gasped, obviously close to a second climax. "Oh!"

He'd reached the S's, and was losing hope fast. "Spiny

Orb-Weaver," he muttered under a ragged breath.

"What?" She laughed a little, and then sobbed her release.

Nate finally let go, pouring himself into her as he held her close in his arms. She was still breathing fast, her face buried in the crook of his neck. Withdrawing gently, after the single-most incredible sex of his life, he turned and fell onto the bed beside her.

Closing his eyes, he concentrated on breathing and getting his heartrate back into its normal range. She stirred beside him, letting out a purr of satisfaction that made him open one eye. She was staring at him, her eyes deep and her mouth curved in a smile. His heart, now more or less back to itself, gave a thump that he doubted had anything to do with sex.

"What are you thinking, Becks?"

She trailed one hand up his arm and then touched his cheek. "I'm thinking Bugs Bauer is pretty darn good in the sack."

That made his laugh a little. "I'm glad you enjoyed it, but I have a confession to make."

She screwed up her face in mock confusion. "You have

a bug fetish? Makes sense."

He chuckled and slid his hand down to her round butt to give one cheek a pinch. "Not even close."

She giggled and leaned up on one elbow, resting her head on her hand. "Tell me, Bugs."

"I have to say this surpassed even my fantasies, Becks."

She blinked, her lips parted. "You mean, since high school?"

"No, baby." He kissed her nose, and then her lips. "I had no clue about sex in high school. I meant the fantasies I've been having since I saw you behind that giant plant at your desk on my first day."

Laughing, she kissed him. "You had me worried there."

"About my teenage fantasies?"

"Oh, no. About that spider you were talking about."

He flushed a little and shrugged. "That was just a way to delay the inevitable."

"Then I shouldn't worry about you dumping me for a girl with eight legs?"

Laughing out loud, he gathered her in his arms once more.

Sometime later, he drove back to the house in St. Cloud.

It wouldn't be long before he could just walk across the hall after being with Becky. It was a cozy situation, even if it could get complicated.

"I won't let it," he vowed to himself.

The house was dark when he got there, and the note he found in the kitchen confirmed his suspicions that she was out with the stink bug. It kind of sucked, because he'd wanted to talk to her about their upcoming changes in living situations.

He was pleasantly wrung out from his time in Becky's bed, so he jumped in the shower and then pulled on a pair of sweatpants. Settling on the fat leather couch he thought he'd get in the big move, he flicked on the TV. He didn't see much of the soccer game he'd found on the high channels, as his mind kept going back to what had happened with Becks.

She was amazing. Just touching her skin made him all kinds of turned on, and finally having her? It was beyond any expectations. That bit he'd divulged about the spiders was a little embarrassing, though.

"I can't believe I said that out loud," he grumbled. "What an idiot."

Tomorrow he was going to the famous Chapman barbecue. With Becky, as everybody seemed to expect. It didn't matter. She was his, for now. Hell, for as long as he could make this thing last. The rest of it? The complications, the inevitable expectations he won't be able to meet?

He would just wrap up those thoughts tighter than an Orb-weaver's web and hope that he didn't end up tangled in it before all was said and done.

***

Becky caught herself humming all throughout the morning. After taking a long leisurely bath at her place, a welcome departure from her usual Sunday morning trip to the inn for cinnamon rolls and inquisitions from her mother, she dressed for the Chapman barbecue. A pair of denim shorts, a faded pink vintage T showcasing an old-timey canoe tour and her favorite black Chuck Taylors. She couldn't help but wonder what Nate was up to this morning. Was he as blissfully tired as she was?

Kudos went to him for diving headlong into the family event this afternoon. Harmony was really turning into Lettie 2.0 with her matchmaking.

"Match is already set, Harmony," Becky murmured.

Not that she'd wanted that so quickly. Kent's dumping last year still stung, but she recognized that was due more to her pride getting hurt than her heart. What she felt for Nate was on a whole new level. She'd been half in love with him in high school, but that hadn't gone very far. Now? Now she was in danger of falling for the guy.

The sunlight was bright through the slats of her window blinds, so she slathered on the sunblock. Freckles might be her fate as a Rollins, but her skin didn't have to be bright red along with her hair. She pulled her hair into a high ponytail, since Nate was going to pick her up in his truck. No bike ride this morning.

After that second round in her bed, they'd talked about just how they would handle today's inevitably-close scrutiny. She'd schooled him on the Chapman's long history of weekly picnics, although she'd also pointed out that she'd managed to avoid any of the usual snares their hostess tended to set.

Harmony might claim that she had no ulterior motives, but Becky couldn't argue with the happy unions of Jake and Claire Chapman and Ty and Cassie Walsh, not to mention Ben and Tammy Chapman. Becky wasn't sure how she felt about everyone finding out about her and Nate, but there was no getting out of it now. Bugs sure was a good sport, but she'd always known that about him. The other stuff? The steamy, naughty stuff? That was a completely delightful surprise.

She tucked her phone into her bag, grabbed the bottle of Moscato she'd bought at the market from the fridge, and then headed out into the hallway. Mrs. Barnes stood there in her housecoat, the Sunday paper in her hand.

"Good afternoon, dear!" the woman said.

Becky smiled at her neighbor. In that pink robe she really looked like Mrs. Potts from Beauty and the Beast.

"I hear you're headed down south pretty soon, Mrs. Barnes."

She nodded, her gray curls bobbing around her face. "I am. Sublet the condo to such a nice young man." Her blue eyes twinkled. "You know him, I think?"

Becky flushed and knew she wore the scarlet stain on her face. At least it wasn't a letter A.

"I do. Nate Bauer is a good man."

Mrs. Barnes winked. "So I heard."

Becky gaped at her and then the woman giggled. "I'm just teasing you, dear. Yesterday Lettie Fairfax was going on about the latest young man to grace Cypress Corners. I'll miss that old girl."

"Boca isn't so far away," Becky said.

"True. I'll have to make sure to come back for the festivals."

"There sure are enough of them, so you'll have your pick."

Mrs. Barnes nodded again. "Maybe I'll treat myself to a stay at your mother's inn, dear. I hear she's going to add a spa?"

This was news to Becky, but leave it to her mother to test the waters before diving in.

"I'm not sure, but that would be a great idea," she said.

"Well, I'm off to do the Jumble and relax for a bit. I have some packing to do, but I feel quite decadent hanging about in my robe."

"Do you need any help? With the packing, that is?"

"You see, Becky? You and that Nate fellow have a lot in common. He offered to help me too."

Becky smiled. "That sure sounds like Nate."

The older woman narrowed her eyes. "You've known the man for some time, haven't you?"

"Since high school."

"And you know him well?"

Becky was tempted to tease the busy body, but stopped short of saying she knew Nate *in the biblical sense*. Instead she nodded.

"Then I feel I can trust him. Although I had good vibes from him yesterday. He seems very conscientious."

She nodded again, hoping this conversation didn't dip into PG-13 territory.

"I'm off to the Chapman barbeque," Becky told her. "Please let me know if you need anything."

"Will do. Have a nice time, dear."

Becky hurried down the stairs, thinking it would be safer waiting for Nate at the little pocket park across from her condo than in the hallway with the inquisitive Mrs. Barnes.

It was a beautiful afternoon, with those big fluffy white clouds crowding together in the bright blue sky. Just as she settled onto a bench set near a gardenia bush, Nate pulled up in his Silverado. As he stepped out, looking pretty hot in a soft gray polo and khaki shorts, she called out to him. He turned, and a big smile wreathed his face.

"What are you doing out here?" he asked as he joined her.

"Waiting for you. Mrs. Barnes is very excited to have

---

you lease her place. Very nosy too, but that's part of her charm."

"The fishbowl?"

"You know it."

He took the wine from her hands and waved her toward the truck. "Then let's dive in. There's no avoiding it."

Her mind worked as she climbed into the truck. "Would you want to avoid it? The gossip, I mean?"

"Becks, it doesn't bother me. You?"

She shrugged. "I'm used to it."

He started the engine. "Let's do this thing. In for a penny."

"In for a pound?" she finished.

"Yep."

"Another of your mother's sayings?"

He nodded. "She has a million of them."

The drive to the Chapmans' house across from the main lakeshore was a short one. Rick and Harmony's house was a gorgeous two-story. The place was situated in one of the more spacious lots of Cypress Corners. The large lot and all of the high-end fixtures should have made the house look grand and off-putting but this home was very welcoming. It was like the inn in that way, balancing aesthetics and amenities with hominess.

It claimed a beautiful view of the central lakeshore across the street, and a deep porch stretched across the front. Adirondack chairs and a hanging bench swing beckoned visitors to the porch enclosed by columns and a railing. The house was painted a dove gray and the roof was peaked slate.

"This place is nice," Nate said as they pulled up to the curb.

"Understatement, but I agree."

He shut off the engine and the two of them soon stood on that wide front porch. Side by side and very close, and Becky's heart thumped. Their relationship, such as it was, would change this afternoon. Through sheer exposure, really.

She rapped on the wooden screen door since the front door was thrown open behind it. The day was going to be a warm one, but for right now Becky guessed that Harmony wanted to take advantage of the fresh breezes that would blow through the house. Becky could hear chatter and laughter from within, picking out a few familiar voices.

"Looks like a full house," she said.

Nate shrugged that off. He really was a good sport.

Harmony came to the door right away, a big grin on her pretty face. "Nate! Becky!" She pushed open the screen door. "Come on in."

Becky and Nate exchanged a look and stepped into the foyer.

In for a penny, indeed.

Chapter 12

Nate stepped into the Sales Center, his mother at his side. She was practically buzzing with excitement this morning and he couldn't help but smile. He hadn't really thought about her wanting her own place so badly. After he and Laura had broken up, it had felt natural to live together. He'd been licking his wounds, and maybe overestimating the amount of help he was to his mother. It was high time he stood on his own two feet. He was coming to realize that this move to Cypress would be good for the both of them.

"Good morning, Nate," Sharon Walsh said from behind the front desk.

Nate smiled at Ty's mother. "Good morning."

Sharon's gaze turned toward Nate's mother. "Hello! You must be Nate's mother. There's so much of you in him."

His mother beamed. "Thank you, yes! I'm Donna."

"Sharon." The women shook hands. "Cassie tells me you and Nate are settling here in Cypress Corners?"

"Cassie?" Nate's mother asked, looking to him for explanation.

"Cassie is Sharon's daughter-in-law, Mom," Nate said.

Sharon laughed lightly. "Yes. Cassie claims she doesn't

care for the fishbowl but she sure doesn't mind feeding the fish."

Nate chuckled at the analogy. "The doc was nice enough to give me some free time to tour with my mom today."

"Oh, how nice! Donna, you're going to love the Active Adult community."

His mother nodded enthusiastically. "Chip has been going on and on about it."

Sharon blinked. "Chip?"

Nate clenched his teeth at the mention of the stink bug. "Chip is my mother's friend," he managed to say.

Sharon's brows drew together, but she didn't ask anything further about him. "Let me tell Eli you're ready for your tour."

Nate nodded and he and his mother stood for a few minutes in the cool air of the center.

"Good morning, Nate!" Oliver sang as he walked into the reception area.

Nate smiled at Oliver. "Morning."

Ollie looked at his mother. "And this must be your sister?"

Nate wasn't surprised to find the guy flirtatious. He sure was a sunny kind of guy. "My mother, Oliver. Donna Bauer."

Ollie dipped his head. "Donna, it's so nice to meet you."

His mother grinned at the pretty guy. "Nice to meet you, Oliver. Oh Nate, everyone is so nice in Cypress! No wonder you've been spending so much time out here."

Oliver laughed. "Yes. Sharon and me? We're the reason Nate is so attached to Cypress."

Nate shook his head. "Never mind."

"Have you taken your mom over to the Institute, Nate?" Ollie asked.

"Not yet."

"Hmm." He turned to Nate's mother. "Donna, you must meet the girl at the front desk. She's a doll."

"Oh, yes!" Sharon put in. "Becky is one of my favorite people."

"Becky?" His mother turned to him. "Nate, who's Becky? Is she the girl that lives across from your new apartment?"

Oliver snickered. "I believe she is, Donna. Nate?"

Nate's lips thinned. He was spared from answering all of the inquiring eyes when Eli Graham joined them.

"Nate, good morning!" Eli was a big guy, with an ever-present smile. "Mrs. Bauer."

"Donna, please," his mother said. "I can't wait to see what you've found for me."

Eli nodded. "Nate gave me an idea of what you're looking for, but I want you to see a couple of the model homes. Ben Chapman designs and Noah Brady's construction."

"You won't find anything better," Nate said. "I've only driven by, though."

Eli's smile widened. "Then let's hit it."

Nate waved his mother out the door in front of him before shooting Ollie a warning glare, which sent the guy into a fit of barely-stifled giggles. Sharon shushed him and Nate followed behind his mother to a golf cart parked along the curb.

They got in and buckled, and Eli pulled away from the curb.

"It's a short ride, but why not go in style?" he asked.

His mother nodded. "Eli, you don't sound like you're from around here."

"I'm not, ma'am. Born and bred in Boston."

His accent was thick and Nate had placed him right away. Becky had told him about how Eli came to Cypress just in time for the Fall Festival almost two years ago. He was married now, to one of Becky's good friends. The pretty blond who ran the bakery. They had a baby too, less than a year old Nate guessed. A cute little thing.

"You came down here and stayed, then?" his mother asked.

"Sure did." He threw her and Nate a wink. "Best thing I've ever done."

"You sure seem happy. Doesn't he seem happy, Nate?"

"He does."

She sighed. "There must be something in the water, because I'm feeling good just riding through the place."

"You have to stop by the bakery, Donna," Eli said. "My wife Caro is always up to something."

"Becky said she's trying a few new things for the Spring Festival?" Nate asked.

"She is. I'm sworn to secrecy. That's the price I pay to be her happy guinea pig."

"Becky?" his mother asked. "There's that name again. Are you close to Becky?"

Nate cleared his throat. "Close?"

She wore a thoughtful expression, and then brightened. "You went to school with a Becky! A pretty redheaded girl, if I remember correctly."

"She sure is," Eli said. "I'm partial to blonds myself. Like my wife and our sweet mini-cupcake."

"You have a baby," his mother gushed. "How wonderful! Nate, isn't that wonderful?"

"It is." Nate kept his focus on his hands as they rounded the bend toward the Active Adult section. He wouldn't put it past his mother to bring up the subject of grandchildren. She hadn't mentioned it since his breakup, but today was a new day wasn't it? And folks kept bringing up Becks, with raised brows no less.

"There it is," Eli said with a lift of his chin.

Nate's mother was soon distracted by the rows of treelined streets leading to Craftsman style bungalows. From the documents Eli had sent over last week, Nate knew most of them were one-stories built to resemble two-stories. The effect was pleasing and homey.

"Oh, Nate." Her voice was thick as she grabbed onto Nate's arm. "Isn't it lovely?"

Nate smiled at his mother and gave her shoulders a squeeze. This was good. This was exactly what she needed.

And what he needed, too.

***

Becky busied herself with any number of necessary tasks at her desk on Monday. She and Nate had spent most of yesterday together, first at the picnic and then in her bed. She'd caught a glimpse of Nate and his mother across the street an hour earlier, and couldn't help but hope that they would find a place for her. Nate was moving into Mrs. Barnes apartment at the end of the week, after all. She sucked in a breath. The guy she was seeing was moving in across the hall!

"Morning, Becks!" Harmony sang as she bounced down the hall from her office.

Becky shook her head. "Harmony, you have to stop. Wasn't yesterday enough?"

"Did it bother you, Becky?" Harmony's brows drew together. "Really?"

Becky reached out to touch Harmony's shoulder. "No. Nate and I knew we would be outed once we stepped onto your front porch."

Harmony beamed a smile. "Whew, good."

"And I have to admit, Rick sure knows how to cook meat."

Harmony laughed. "The man never seems to get tired of it." She propped a hip on the edge of Becky's desk. "Nate's mom is moving out here too, huh?"

"I think that's the plan."

She crossed her arms. "Rick told me there are several places available for quick move-in."

Becky nodded. "Oliver said something about that."

"You know, that community is pretty far from your condo."

"Yes." *Hmm.* "It is."

"And Nate will be just across the hall?"

"Yes," Becky said again.

Harmony stared at her for a long minute.

"Harmony, what are you getting at?"

Harmony let out a breath. "Becky, I know about you and Nate."

Becky leveled a look at her. "Harmony, everybody knows about me and Nate."

Harmony leaned closer. "I mean, before."

Becky's heart gave a thump. "Did Joy tell you?"

Harmony's gaze slid over toward the plant she'd given Becky on her anniversary. "We were talking about…things…and your name came up."

"And she told you we dated?"

Harmony looked at her again. "She told me you two were hot and heavy."

That made Becky smile. "I had no game and he didn't have much more. Hot but not so much heavy."

There was more to what they'd had back then. Becky could admit that. She'd fallen for him and he'd left her without a second glance. But he'd apologized for that, hadn't he? And now they were in an adult relationship.

"You were different people then," Harmony said.

"That's true."

"And he's very different from Kent."

Becky quirked her lips. "No joke."

Harmony placed a hand on her shoulder. "Just trust your heart. You have a good one."

Becky swallowed thickly and managed to shrug. "It's a little early for heart talk, I think."

Harmony did that head-tilt thing, her hazel eyes deep.

"That's what I thought, too."

With that, she left Becky to finish up her work. It was early days. The earliest, actually.

Oliver bounced into the Institute twenty minutes later, his usual smile plastered on his face. "Hey, red! How's it shaking?"

"It's shaking." She swiveled in her chair to face him. "Are you ready for our meeting?"

He held up a glossy green folder with the Cypress Corners logo on the front, and then waved his tablet at her. "Try to stop me."

She laughed. "Okay. Thanks for agreeing to meet over here."

"Hey, you and Nate the Great both work here. Made sense."

She arched a brow. "Nate the Great?"

"Oh, yes." He put on a sorrowful face. "Don't tell me he's not…"

"Oliver!" she cut in, her face hot. "Seriously?"

"As long as he's keeping my girl happy? He's great in my book."

She narrowed her eyes. "Nice save." She stood and

gathered up her stuff. "Let's head into the conference room. Nate can join us there."

Her phone chimed at that second. Glancing at the screen, she saw that Nate had texted her.

My mom loves the place.

Smiling, she answered. *That's great!*

Dropping her at the coffee shop. See you soon.

She responded. *See you soon.*

Oliver clicked his tongue. "Sexting, red?"

She pocketed her phone. "No, wise guy. Let's go."

Oliver gave an dramatic shrug and they both walked down the hall to the conference room. Becky sat at the burlwood table and opened up her notebook and tapped her tablet to life.

"We've covered a lot of ground over the past couple of weeks," she said. "Our booth should be pretty inviting."

"The Sales Center's will be very welcoming. Rick wants to show prospective residents just why they should live here."

"Dr. Robbins sent me his notes," Becky said. "The Institute wants to teach residents and visitors how to live here with nature."

"Knowing you and Harmony, it won't be a boring lecture."

Becky grinned. "Nope. And Lettie is going to help with suggested plants for homeowners."

"Lettie?" Oliver's blue eyes widened. "That should be a hoot and a half. Love that lady."

"We'll make sure to keep her supplied with sweet tea," she joked. "What about the surrey bikes? Any news there?"

Ollie nodded vigorously. His boyfriend Todd ran the sporting goods store on the square, and had recently begun the process of acquiring four-seater surrey bikes to rent by the half hour to residents and visitors.

"Yes! He said he should have a small fleet to rent out during the festival. It will be their launch, he actually said."

Becky winked. "Fleet. Launch. I get it."

Ollie grinned. "Yeah, I think Todd was a sailor in a former life."

"The surreys will keep to the bike paths?" she asked.

"Yes. His proposal was approved. They're considered bikes and don't have to be registered."

"I can't wait to drive one!"

"They're corny and sweet and just about perfect for

Cypress."

"Corny and sweet?" Nate stepped into the conference room. "Sounds about right."

Becky took a long minute to run her gaze over him. He was mussed from his ride out and back to the Active Adult community and his hair was sticking to his temples. His eyes were bright and his smile wide.

"Hey there, Nate the Great," Ollie said.

Nate rolled his eyes. "Oliver." He sat and placed his tablet on the table. "What did I miss?"

Oliver scoffed. "Never mind that. Did you find a place for your mom?"

He glanced at Becky and then back at Oliver. "I did. She's moving in next week."

"So soon?" Becky asked. "How?"

"Rent to own, through the Sales Center," Oliver answered for him. "Eli has special incentives available. Better to use them for one of our own, right?"

Becky watched emotion flicker in Nate's eyes. He was starting to belong in Cypress. That was obvious. She'd known he'd been a great ball player in high school but he was also kind of a bug nerd. That hadn't gained him many friends, other than his teammates. And her, of course.

"I'll be glad to have everything settled," he said, his gaze on her.

She heard Oliver snicker but didn't care.

That tender expression on Nate's face proved to her that he was starting to belong to her, too.

Chapter 13

The day of the festival arrived, and Becky was up before the sun. This was the first year she was the sole point person for the Institute. Though she'd tried to hide it over the past few weeks, she was putting a lot of pressure on herself to make this the best showing ever.

Nate had moved in across the hall, although he spent the night at her place a few times a week. They were getting closer, at least on her side of things. Neither of them talked about the future, though. A month or so into a relationship wasn't the time to raise the topic of commitment. They were exclusive, and that had to be enough for now.

After getting dressed in a crisp camp shirt and khaki shorts, she made a quick cup of coffee. A knock came at her door and, smiling, she put in another coffee pod for Nate.

She let him in and they shared a sweet kiss. He wore a polo with the Institute logo and shorts too.

"Morning, Becks. You ready for today?"

She mentally shook off her apprehension and nodded. "I think so."

He wrapped her in his arms. He smelled so good, and she buried her nose in the hollow at the base of his throat.

"Baby, you got this," he said. "I've never seen anyone with as much attention to detail."

"Thanks."

They parted after another kiss and she made him his coffee, cream no sugar like she knew he took it, and handed it to him.

"The coffee shop won't be open yet."

Nate nodded and sipped. "I bet it'll be a madhouse once it does."

"Caro Graham's bakery, too. They'll open earlier than usual, though. For the vendors."

"I've only tried a couple of things there. My mom loves their scones."

Nate's mom had settled into her house quickly, with her son's help. She'd promised to help out at their booth today, too.

"Tom told me he and Ashlyn have been working overtime to stock the bakery racks."

"Ashlyn?"

"The girl who works there most days. Tom has a thing for her, I think."

"And he's not going to talk to his big sister about it."

"Nope."

They finished their coffee and headed down to Nate's truck. He took the few bins she'd had at home with more handouts and other material she'd been working on, and they set out for the square. The road would be blocked to all but foot traffic within the hour, so they parked behind the Institute. Booths were being set up, canopies beginning to line the square on all four sides. Harmony was already out front, with little Nick.

"Hi, Becky!" the seven-year-old called.

"Hi there, Nick." Becky gave him a hug. "You ready for today, big guy?"

Nick grinned, showing a wide gap in his smile. "I love the festival."

"We could sure use the help," Nate said. "You're going to help me with the bug presentations, right?"

Nick's eyes widened. "Yeah, I am! Max is gonna be jealous, I'll bet."

Max was Noah and Jessie Brady's little boy, and Nick's best friend.

"That's not nice," Harmony said. "Besides, Max gets to go on the tours today."

Nick shrugged. "I guess that's cool, too." He brightened. "Maybe Uncle Ty can take me out later."

"Let's slow our jets, little man," Rick said as he joined them from across the street. "We have a long day ahead of us."

Becky and Nate started setting up as Rick talked about what the Sales Center was going to do today. The place was closed, as was usual on the weekends, but they would do tours.

"Is the bakery open yet?" Rick asked.

"Caro almost always opens early on festival days," Harmony said. "I'll head over and see."

"Let me." Nate straightened and turned, bumping right into Ashlyn. "Sorry."

The girl laughed and held up a bakery box in Sweet Escape's trademark bright green. "Caro sent me. With provisions."

Harmony clasped her hands together. "Love that girl!" She took the box and set it on the nearest table. "Becky, you have to see these."

Inside the box were pink-frosted pastries the size of a jar lid. They were plump, and the dough looked like a biscuit dotted with red.

"What are those?" Becky asked Ashlyn.

"Strawberry shorties." She winked. "I came up with the name."

Ashlyn dropped a cute curtsey and hurried back to the bakery. The treats were delicious, and they all fell on them. Not much was said as they devoured the pastries, which tasted like crisp strawberry shortcakes. Nick's face was covered in icing and Nate's was only a little bit cleaner.

"Eli was right," Nate said as he wiped his mouth. "His wife is an amazing baker."

"She's teaching my brother and Ashlyn the ropes, too," Becky said.

"How old is Ashlyn?" he asked.

"Not sure. Twenty-two maybe," she said.

"Why?" Harmony asked.

Nate shook his head. "I don't know. She looks familiar but she's too young to have gone to school with us," he said to Becky.

After a visit to Cool Beans to grab a couple of cups of what Nate called "real coffee" they were just about ready for the festival to begin. The sky was a bright blue and the clouds were placed just right. There was a light breeze, but she knew the day would be very warm.

She took a few moments to drink in the moment, working with Nate and doing what she loved. With the people she cared about, too. She caught Nate's smile in her direction and her earlier fears seemed to fade.

"You ready, Becks?" he asked.

She couldn't keep the smile from her face. "Bring it on."

***

Nate held the secure plastic box in front of the wide-eyed children. "This is a Spined Soldier Bug," he told them. "A very beneficial insect."

"Beany what?" Nick Chapman asked.

"Beneficial," Nate said. "That means it's very useful to farmers and gardeners." He scrunched up his face in an attempt to look vicious. "It fights off the bugs that otherwise might destroy fruits and vegetables. And the plants in your yard, too."

He placed the box on his lap and they all leaned in to take a closer look. The bugs inside, each about half an inch long, marched over and around the twigs and leaves inside

159

like their namesake.

"What are those pointy things on their backs?" a little girl asked.

"Those help you identify these guys as predatory bugs." More wrinkled little brows met his words. "That means they eat those bugs that damage the plants I was talking about."

Oohs and aahs came from the kids.

"They're also a kind of stink bug," he said in a near-whisper.

"Stink!" one boy said. "Ha!"

The other kids giggled and made eww sounds at that revelation. Grinning, Nate slowly shook his head. "You know, even the cute little ladybug has the same defense. They let out a stink to scare away their own predators and to let other stink bugs know there's danger."

"That's cool," another little girl said.

"It is," Nate said with a nod. "Now, this spiny guy here is different from most stink bugs you might find."

"How?" Nick asked him.

"Some of them, a lot of them, aren't helpful like these guys."

"Why?" Nick asked.

An image of his mother's friend Chip came into his head and he fought back a laugh. "Most stink bugs are all about eating fruits and vegetables and ruining plants."

"Oh, bad bugs!" a blond boy declared.

"Yep!" Nate said. "You nailed it, buddy."

The kid beamed a smile. As he and the other kids watched the Soldier Bugs, Nate caught Becky watching him. Her arms were crossed and she wore the sweetest look on her pretty face. His heart thumped as he caught not just approval but something else in her expression. Affection, heat and maybe more.

Before he could give more than a second to thoughts about that subject, he turned to the next subject of his presentation. As he explained the benefits of the cute little ladybugs to his rapt audience, he felt a shift inside. A sense of belonging that had niggled at the back of his consciousness since his very first day in Cypress. A sense of home.

Just a few hours later, the Spring Festival was in the books. The Institute's booth had been busy most of the day, and Becky had fielded so many questions he'd wondered if there was anything she didn't know.

"Boy, I'm beat," she said as she packed up what few

programs and literature were left. "It went well though, right?"

He leveled a look at her. "Are you kidding? You killed it."

Her gaze dipped to her feet before meeting his again. "I didn't do it alone, Bugs."

He chuckled. "Speaking of…" He waved a hand toward the insect cases chilling in the shade of the canopy. "I have to go release these guys."

"Good bugs," she said. "I caught a few of your presentations. You rocked it."

"It was a lot of fun. I admit, I was nervous at first."

"Kids can be the toughest audience."

"I had them at Stink Bug," he joked.

"No offense, but they aren't as cute as the ladybugs."

"Insect bias." He clicked his tongue. "I see it every day."

She laughed and came closer. "What can I say? They're little redheads. I feel an affinity."

The heat of the day heightened her sweet scent and he longed in that second to hold her close and just breathe her in. He settled for a kiss on the top of her head. "What are your dinner plans, Becks?"

She pulled back, an wary expression on her face. "I kind of promised your mom that we would have dinner with her and her friend Chip in the tavern."

"The Stink Bug," he grumbled. "And not the good kind."

"Yeah, he seems a little…plastic."

"I saw him talking Lettie up during her presentation."

"Lettie doesn't suffer fools, Nate. She shut him down in a 'bless your heart' kind of way."

"I knew I liked that lady."

"She sure likes you. Or, likes you for me."

"What about you, Becks?" He arched a brow. "Do you like me for you?"

It was an offhanded question, but one that could be taken a couple of ways. Becky seemed to take it at face value as she came up on her toes to kiss him.

"I really do, Bugs."

Harmony cleared her throat to his left and they stepped apart.

"Why don't you two go ride the surrey bikes? Todd's going to extend the service for today. Until seven."

Nate smiled at Becky, who clasped her hands. "Are you sure, Harmony? I don't want to leave everything on your shoulders."

"Becky, you went above and beyond today." She grinned. "Besides, I have my husband and Nick to fetch and carry."

"Sounds good," Nate said. "And thanks."

It seemed natural to take Becky's hand in his as they walked down to the sporting goods store a few storefronts away. The surrey bikes were a big hit today, but the funny vehicles with their four wicker-like seats each with their own set of pedals, not to mention their fringed canopies, weren't exactly his usual mode of transportation.

"Hey, there!" Todd, a dark-haired guy who was as bright and friendly as Oliver, hugged Becky. "Becky, I can't believe you waited until now to try one of these babies out." He stood back and eyed Nate up and down. "Nate the Great, I presume?"

Nate chuckled. "According to Oliver."

Todd tipped his head to the side. "Not according to Becky?" He pouted. "That's sad."

Becky elbowed him. "Never mind. Do you have a bike

we can use?"

Todd smiled again. "Of course."

There was a lime green surrey parked at the curb. This one has a striped canopy and looked absolutely ridiculous. When Becky climbed in and perched her Chuck Taylors on the pedals, though? Nate thought it was just about right.

He dipped his head in thanks to Todd and got in beside her. "You ready to do this?"

"Have you ever driven one of these?"

"Not even once. You?"

She nodded. "They used to have these on the boardwalk by the beach. Mom, Dad, Joy and me would all pedal while Tom sat in one of these front seats."

The surrey had what looked like baby seats tacked to front of it. "I can't imagine your brother ever being that small."

"Right? Dad used to tease him all the time. Called him 'peewee' even as he was obviously growing taller by leaps and bounds."

He caught the wistfulness in her voice. "He sounds like he was a fun dad."

"He was."

165

Nate usually swallowed the regret at never knowing his own dad, but it unexpectedly hit him today. They began to pedal the surrey and he was happy to hide his preoccupation with the easy exercise. As they rode through the square and up toward the lakeshore, he couldn't help but wonder who his father was. If he'd been in Nate's life, would he be a different guy now? Hell, would he have been a better kid back when he'd first dated Becky? He didn't know, and never would.

"Isn't this a hoot?" she asked him, her breath coming fast.

He agreed with a smile. He couldn't go back in time. He couldn't un-ring a bell. But he could do his damnedest to make the best out of the life he had now.

Steering the surrey toward a copse of trees, he threw her a wink. Her eyes lit with answering heat and his smile widened. A little make-out session in the shade was just what he needed to forget about the past and focus on the present.

Chapter 14

The dining room at the Clubhouse was just as Becky remembered it. Crisp linen tablecloths, cut crystal stemware, numerous silver utensils set on either side of each plate. It was a long time since she'd had dinner there. It was on the occasion of her parents' anniversary soon after they'd all moved to Cypress Corners. Their last anniversary, actually.

She'd come here a few times since, of course. For meetings and a few lunches with Dr. Robbins over the years. This dinner with Nate and his mother, though? It was elegant and fine and slightly uncomfortable. Donna Bauer was a lovely woman, and Becky had liked her from the time they'd first met weeks ago. But this Chip guy? He seemed smarmy, and his smile was way too big.

They'd avoided having dinner with the older couple after the festival, and she had no regrets on that count. After their stolen kisses on the surrey bike, neither of them had wanted anything else but to head back to her condo. That was then and this was now, and it had been a week since the festival. She let Nate talk her into coming to dinner with them, but that was only during pillow talk Friday night. She was a sucker for his pillow talk, and a lot of other things he did to her on those pillows.

"We are enjoying your Cypress Corners, Becky," Chip said with a wink. "Although it's starting to feel like *our* Cypress Corners, isn't that right Donna?"

"You're not wrong there, Chip." Nate's mom smiled in the guy's direction. "It feels like home."

Nate stiffened. "Home? Are you living out here, Chip?"

Chip let out a loud laugh. "Not yet, my boy."

Becky glanced at Nate to find his expression set.

"I'm not your boy," he stated.

"Nate, honey!" Donna said, placing her hand on Nate's arm. "Chip was just being folksy."

"I was just being folksy," Chip parroted.

Nate's eyes held ice Becky had never seen before, and she shifted in her seat. He did not like this guy, or what he was becoming to his mother. That was as crystal clear as their water glasses.

The sommelier came by with the bottle of wine Chip requested, giving them all a welcome breather. The man poured Chip's glass first, and Chip made a show of sampling it. Becky doubted he had any clue about the wine's quality despite his sucking sounds and rolling eyes. Then he nodded and wine was poured for the rest of them. Nate downed his in a few gulps, another indication that he was definitely not himself tonight.

Things didn't improve as they ate dinner. The meal was impeccable, and Becky's salmon was possibly the best she'd ever eaten. She also knew the price of the dish, so she wasn't going to waste it. Nate barely touched his lamb chops, though. After that first downed glass of wine he didn't have anything else to drink but water.

At the end of the meal, Chip announced that he had to make a call. After giving Donna a loud wet kiss on the back of her hand, he stood and bowed to Becky before heading out into the lobby. Donna watched him go with stars in her eyes, but Becky wasn't fooled. She'd dated enough jerks to pick up just what Chip had put down.

"Oh, isn't he just the most gallant of men?" Donna gushed.

Becky was spared coming up with any kind of answer to that when Nate spoke.

"You know he's not coming back, right?"

His mother's eyes rounded. "Nate, what do you mean?"

"I mean, he never had any intention of paying for his

own meal let alone ours."

Donna shook her head. "No. No! This was Chip's idea.
He wanted us all to get to know each other better." She
looked imploringly at Becky. "Becky, you and Nate are so
close now. I think Chip wants that for us too. Don't you?"

Becky chose her words carefully, hyperaware of Nate's
watching her. "Mrs. Bauer, I…"

"Donna, dear. Please."

Becky inclined her head. "Donna. I don't feel I know
Chip well enough to answer that question."

"I do." Nate leaned over to grab his wallet out of his
back pocket. "He's a user. And it pisses me off that you can't
see that he's using *you*."

Donna gaped at him, and then her eyes filled with
visible tears. "Nate, how can you say that to me?"

Nate signaled for the server and handed her his credit
card. "Because I've seen this before, Mom." The check
arrived and Nate signed it with jagged motions. "What gets
me is that you never see it." He stood. "Never."

His mother stood, dabbing her eyes with the fine linen
napkin. "If that's how you feel—"

Becky held up her hands. "Let's not talk about this

now," she rushed out. "This is something the two of you have to hash out in private."

Nate was clearly steaming, but he seemed to agree with her. "I'll take you home, since the stink bug won't be back any time soon."

"Stink bug?!" Donna's voice rose to an octave Becky hadn't heard since those long-ago teenage arguments she'd had with her sister. "Nate!"

"Enough." Nate's voice was cold now. "Let's get out of here."

Becky and Donna preceded Nate out the grand doorway of the Clubhouse, neither saying anything as Nate drove his mother back to her house.

"Good night, Nate." Donna stepped down from the truck and then squared her shoulders and lifted her chin. "When you're ready to apologize, you know where I am."

"Good night," was all Nate said.

He said nothing else as they drove back to the condo. Becky had never seen him like this, so closed off. He parked behind the building and turned off the engine. Reaching over to him, she touched his tightened fist on the steering wheel. He sucked in a breath, and his broad shoulders appeared to

171

relax a fraction.

"I'm sorry," he bit out.

"No need to apologize." She thought about what she considered their song. "Good thing, because it's too late."

He glanced at her and, after a second, a smile broke across his face. "You're too good for me, Becks."

No one had ever said that to her before. Not even Kent at his smarmiest. "There's no such thing, Bugs. You deserve all good things."

He pulled her against him and kissed her hard. "Let's get upstairs. Your place, my place. I don't care."

"How about yours?" she breathed.

Nodding, he all but pulled her up the stairs and they soon tumbled onto his bed. He touched her, caressed her, and never stopped kissing her. He seemed almost frantic and her pulse pounded as he easily roused her passions to match his. That was saying something, because he was almost fierce.

"Tell me, Becks." His mouth ran over her breasts, her belly. Her center. "Tell me you're mine?"

He'd never asked for that before, and she couldn't deny him the truth that was in her heart. "Yes, I'm yours."

***

Nate brought his face to hers then, their breath mingling as they both panted. "You're mine." He kissed her. "God, you're mine."

Her admission meant everything to him right then. After that disastrous dinner with the stink bug, and his argument with his mother, he needed Becks more than ever. Stroking her silken skin, tasting the hint of salty sweetness of her flesh, he wanted only her. He had to be inside her.

Without another thought, he entered her. They moved together, sweet and hot and perfect. It was fast. It was overwhelming. When she reached her peak with a reedy cry and he came deep inside of her? It was like he was finally home.

Something niggled at the back of his mind, though. About something he'd never done in his whole adult life.

Collapsing on the bed beside her, he squeezed his eyes shut. "Damn it."

Becky let out a breath and turned to him. "Not what you usually say, Bugs."

He opened his eyes again and faced her. "I didn't use a condom."

Her full lips parted. "Oh." Then she waved a hand. "I

173

think we're okay."

He sat up, scrubbing his hands over his face. "I'm sorry, Becks."

She stretched out on top of him. "You can make up for it, you know."

A smile played around her lips and his heart thumped. "Yeah?"

She nodded. "Use one this time."

Just like that, heat flared and he lost himself in her again.

The next morning he put aside the shit show that had been last night's dinner. He'd left Becky sleeping in his bed and driven to the square. The streets were a little on the quiet side this Sunday morning, but the bakery was hopping as usual.

"Good morning, Nate!" Caro Graham said with a wave of her hand.

Nate nodded at Eli's wife. "Good morning. What's good today?"

Caro laughed and the familiar young woman he'd spotted at the festival last week shook her head.

"Everything is good," the girl said.

Nate studied her face. Where did he know her from? "Thanks…"

"Ashlyn," she said with a nod.

"Ashlyn is the best," Caro said. "After Jane, of course."

"You know that's right," said another woman's voice from the back of the shop.

Caro shook her head. The atmosphere in the bakery was light and bright despite the line of customers. He willingly joined that line, though.

When he reached the counter he paused.

"What will it be, Nate the Great?" Caro asked him.

Nate rolled his eyes. "God save me from Oliver. How about a few of those strawberry shorties?"

She nodded. "Coffee? Or are you getting Becky something fancy from next door?"

He blinked. "This whole fishbowl thing can still surprise me."

"Get used to it," Ashlyn said as she wiped down a nearby table. "I might be just a minnow, but I feel it too."

That made him laugh. He stopped in the coffee shop afterwards and then headed for home. As he let himself into the condo he could hear the shower running. Just the thought

175

of Becky's smooth, rosy skin all lathered up and he felt that lick of desire that was never too far below the surface.

He sat at the raised counter and sipped his coffee as he waited for Becky. Last night's events were all jumbled in his head. First that dinner with the stink bug, then the argument with his mother. And later? When he'd forgotten himself with Becky? He was a clod. Luckily she was as forgiving as she was beautiful.

"Hey there, Bugs." She ran her fingers through her damp hair as she joined him. "What have you been up to?"

"Went to the bakery, Becks." He tapped on the bright green paper bag. "Strawberry shorties."

Her eyes widened and an adorable smile spread across her face. "Oh, yay!"

She hopped onto the stool next to him and dug in. She was dressed, more or less, in one of his big T-shirts. Her long legs were bare as were her feet. He could look at her all day, and then do a lot more than just look.

"How are you today?" she asked after taking a few bites.

"Okay." He took a second to sip more of his coffee. "I'm really sorry about last night."

"That's a pretty broad topic." She arched a brow. "About what, exactly?"

That made him smile. "Right? About everything, I guess."

"Nate, you're not responsible for that horrific dinner last night. The salmon was great, by the way. Thank you."

"I'm responsible for what happened after."

"Your discussion with your mom? No worries. I used to live with mine up until a few months ago, Nate. I totally get it."

"We don't argue, Becks. We never have."

"Never?"

He nodded.

"That's surprising," she said. "I have no clue what that's like."

"You argue with your mother a lot?"

"Not now, no. But we're not a family that holds on to things, either. We talk it out." She smiled. "We seldom have an unexpressed thought."

He thought about that. "I don't ever want to have another argument with her like that again."

"What about the stink bug?"

177

"I'll just bite my tongue."

"Whoa." She placed a hand on his. "That's not healthy, Bugs."

"It's what I've bene doing for years, Becky. It's what works."

She shrugged, but thankfully didn't press him further on that. There was the other thing to discuss, though.

"Now, about the other?" he began.

"Don't worry about it, Nate. I'm not."

He let out the breath he'd barely been aware he was holding. "Okay, good."

She tilted her head to one side. "You take on a lot."

"Maybe."

They ate their breakfast and didn't speak any more about last night. He was happy to set it aside. Put a pin in it, like a bug on a board.

It was what he did best, after all.

Chapter 15

Becky let herself into the inn on Tuesday night, guilt niggling at her. She'd been absent from these family dinners for weeks now, almost since she'd started seeing Nate. He was having dinner at his mother's tonight too, without Chip if the guy knew what was good for him.

In the week and a half since that horrid dinner, Nate had seemed resigned to his mother's relationship. He certainly never broached the subject of Chip the stink bug and his mom, and if Becky asked him anything about it he shut her down fast. She sure wasn't going to pick that hill to die on, so she let him keep that aspect of his life to himself.

"Hi, Mom!" she called, setting her bag on the hall table.

The inn was done in Old Florida style, with columns and alcoves painted in creams and whites. A sweeping staircase drew the eye upward to the gallery that led to the guest rooms. Potted palms and nautical touches, along with watercolors done in the style of the Highwaymen, added to the charm. Upstairs the rooms were all sleek and modern, though. The family rooms? Simple and homey, and Becky could acknowledge that she missed living here a little bit.

"Honey!" Her mother came into the lobby, her arms

outstretched. "I've missed you, sweetheart. And now you're here on a Family Tuesday."

Tuesdays were the only day that there was no evening reception set up in the parlor for the inn's guests. Ever since they'd built it, Tuesday nights were for family. It had been their father's idea and their mother upheld the tradition.

Becky hugged her tightly, feeling like a little kid and not caring a thing about that. "Hi, Mom." She pulled back. "It's not like I've been on the moon, you know."

Her mother clicked her tongue. "You've been so busy, Becky. With your job and your young man."

Becky met her mother's inquisitive gaze evenly. "Maybe I have."

"You know, you could have invited him to dinner," her mother said.

"Thanks, but he's eating with his mother tonight."

Lacing her arm through one of Becky's, her mother led her into the dining area. "I've met Donna. She's a lovely woman."

"She is."

Her mother paused in the doorway, her brows knit. "I'm not too sure about her gentleman."

Becky just shrugged. Chip wasn't someone she would talk about, not when Nate wasn't here. Not that she could talk about him when Nate was.

"Hey, girl." Joy sat at the table, her handsome cowboy seated beside her.

"Hi." Becky leaned down and gave Joy a one-armed hug and a kiss on the cheek before rubbing Zach's shoulder. "How are you, Zach?"

"Busy." He grinned. "The stables are getting pretty popular, not to mention taking care of those little horses out at Billy's place."

Joy jabbed her thumb in Zach's direction. "I told him they should have had pony rides at the festival, but I was voted down."

"Little horses, babe," Zach said. "Not ponies. And I don't think they would have enjoyed that."

Joy rolled her eyes. "What have you been up to, little sis?"

Becky sat across from them. "Same old, same old. Work has gotten a little quiet, now that the festival is over."

"And how's Nate?" Zach asked. "I keep wanting to invite him out for a beer but I haven't gotten the chance."

"I'm sure he'd like to hang out," Becky said.

Zach straightened. "You know, I might give him a call about something else."

Joy clasped her hands. "The kids? That's a great idea!"

"Aside from the relationship-speak," Becky began, "I think I'm picking up what you're putting down. The riding lessons?"

Zach shook his head. "I've been helping out with the kids, Becky. Coaching them."

Becky caught on. "Baseball."

He smiled again. "Yep.

"I bet Nate would love that," Becky said. "Pitching?" she teased.

Zach chuckled. "We'll have to fight over the mound, but maybe."

"Oh, you could do that thing with the bat," Becky said. "You know, one hand over the over?"

"Yes!" Joy said. "Oh, do that!"

Zach rolled his eyes now. "Girls."

"Are they giving you a hard time, bro?" Tom said as he joined them.

Becky smiled at their brother. "Hey, Tom."

"Hey, Becky." He dug into the filled-to-overflowing basket of yeast rolls on the table. "What's up, Joy?" he asked with a full mouth of bread.

"Manners, bro," Joy said. "Zach was talking about coaching baseball with Nate."

Tom made a sound of agreement as he swallowed. "Nate was a star on the mound, Zach."

Zach gave a crooked smile. "So was I."

Becky held up her hands. "No need for a peeing contest," she laughed as she stood. "I'm going to help Mom."

Her mother waved her away when she got to the kitchen but Becky grabbed a platter anyway.

"The chops look great," she said.

"I used that indoor grill thing," her mother said. "It sucks the air down or something."

Becky just nodded and they were all soon eating pork chops and a vegetable casserole from a recipe her mother vowed she would take to the grave.

As if it was predetermined, Joy and Becky both helped their mother clean up after everyone was done.

"This is too familiar," Joy joked as they wiped down the table.

"I don't mind," Becky said. "I haven't been here in weeks, so I figure I owe Mom at least this."

They worked in concert to rinse dishes and load the dishwasher.

"So things seem great with you and Nate," Joy began.

"They are."

Joy stopped and crossed her arms. "What aren't you telling me?"

Becky couldn't put her finger on what was bugging her about Nate at the moment, and the tangled mess of his mother's love life and his never knowing his dad was too personal to share with her sister.

"Nothing, Joy. Things are great, just like you said."

Joy's eyes narrowed, eyes a lot like Becky's. Her sister's stare was just as relentless too.

Ignoring Joy's silent order to fess up, Becky focused on their task. She wasn't even sure where, exactly, she and Nate were headed. She sure as heck didn't want to talk about it with her happily-attached big sister.

***

Nate sat and finished his meal, a plate piled generously with his mother's pot roast and potatoes, nodding at the proper places and making sounds of noncommittal agreement now and then. To him she seemed even more vocal than usual, talking about the events planned for her community and everyone she was starting to get to know.

"I've been making friends in Cypress, Nate," she said. "Sharon Walsh is so sweet, and that Lettie! Oh, she's a card."

"I'm with you there."

He waited for her to extol the virtues of Chip the Stink bug but apparently he wasn't part of the conversation just yet.

"Most of the people here are around my age, maybe a little older like sixty. The activities director is just a doll! Nate, if you weren't with Becky I would set the two of you up on a date."

Nate chuckled. "Another reason for me to be glad I'm with Becky."

She took up his empty plate and set it in the sink. He drank his iced tea as she fussed around him. If he were being honest, he kind of missed this. It had been just the two of them for years, after all.

"And there is this older couple, maybe in their late seventies, who you would think were high school sweethearts!" she said.

Nate just nodded again.

"They are so sweet, always so attentive to each other." She paused and let out a sigh. "I never had that."

Nate took another sip of his iced tea and placed the glass on the table. "Never?"

She waved a hand. "Well, not never. Your father and I…"

He stared at her, his heart pounding. "My father?"

"Never mind," she rushed out.

She got up and hurried around the kitchen, straightening things that looked pretty straight already to him.

"Mom, you never talk about him."

"And I never will." Her back was to him as she washed something in the sink, but he could see that her shoulders were hiked up practically to her ears and her back was ramrod stiff. "I've told you before, he left us and that was that."

Nate was damn sure *that* wasn't *that*, but he'd never pressed her for answers before. Maybe it was high time he did.

"What was your relationship like?" he asked, aiming for easygoing with his tone of voice.

Her shoulders dipped a fraction and she turned to face

him. Her smile was bright, but didn't appear forced like he'd seen before. No, she was clearly remembering a time when she was very happy.

"He was such a nice man, Nate. Life just dealt us cards we couldn't play."

"What cards?"

"Nate, honey. Your father and I just weren't meant to be together. That's all. We tried."

"When?"

She blinked. "What?"

"When, Mom? When did you try?"

She bit her lip, her gaze sliding away from his. "You were very little, Nate. We got back together, and I was so happy!"

He worked his mind around that piece of information, not able to recall any guy who stuck around long enough when he was a kid. Several were around for a few weeks, he guessed. He couldn't really be sure of the amount of time, not then and not in retrospect. Had one of those guys been his father?

"Who was this deadbeat?"

"He wasn't a deadbeat! He paid child support up until

the time you turned eighteen."

This was brand new information for him, but he ignored it to focus on the more important questions.

"Who was he?" he asked.

"Nate, it doesn't matter."

He slammed a hand on the table, causing the ice to rattle in their glasses. "It sure as hell matters to me."

Her mouth dropped open and she settled down at the table. She looked a little scared, so he sucked in a breath and held it for a few seconds before slowly letting it out.

"I'm sorry, Mom. I just want to know something, anything, about him."

"He played baseball."

This was a shocker. "What?"

"When I first met him it was during spring training."

Lots of professional ball clubs held their spring training in Florida. Central Florida, Tampa, on the east coast.

"What team did he play for?"

She shook her head. "He didn't. Something about his shoulder. He was on the farmer team for a while, though."

"Farm club," Nate corrected. "Which team?"

"I'm not sure."

"He didn't get called up?" She looked at him blankly and he added. "To the majors?"

"No. He washed out, or whatever it's called." She gave him a small smile now. "He was a pitcher, like you."

The floor seemed to drop out beneath him. His father played baseball. He'd been a pitcher just like Nate.

"I can't believe this," he mumbled.

"Nate, I'm sorry."

He could read the regret clear on her face, and tamped down the urge to lose it on her. "Why can't I know who he is?"

"I promised him."

"You promised him," he repeated. "You promised him!? I'm your son!"

She burst into tears, seemingly out of nowhere. Covering her face with her hands, she sobbed.

"I'm sorry," she said again.

Alarmed, Nate got up and came around to her side of the table. "Don't cry, Mom."

It was what he'd done every time another guy broke her heart. Probably from the time he was little, since his memories stretched as far back as they could. Had he

189

comforted her when his father left that second time?

"I'm sorry I yelled."

She looked up, swiping at her tears. "I'm not crying because you yelled, Nate. You have every right to be angry with me. It's Chip!"

He pulled back. "Chip? What does that dick have to do with this?" His breath caught. "God, don't tell me he's my father."

She shook her head. "No, no." Sniffing, she looked up at him. "He cheated on me."

"Chip cheated on you?" Her lower lip quivered and he tried to think of ways to stem the further onslaught of tears. "I'm sorry he hurt you."

"Why should he be any different from any other man in my life?" She patted his hand. "Except for my beautiful boy."

Nate sat back down, the burden of what he had to do falling over his shoulders. "What do you want me to do?"

"Please stay here with me, Nate?"

"Mom, I can't."

"You can! I cleared it with the homeowners association. Since I qualify by my age, you can stay here."

"That wasn't what I meant."

She looked at him in question. He didn't *want* to live with her again. He was happy living on his own, close to Becky. What the hell would this do to their new relationship?

"Please, Nate? I don't know what I'll do without you."

"You were doing just fine on your own, Mom. You'll be just fine now."

"No." Her mouth was set. "No, I won't be."

"You have friends here. You were just telling me how much fun you're having."

"No," she said again. "They all know what Chip did. That he tossed me aside to go after that widow who moved in last week."

"So who cares?"

"I care!"

He held up his hands. "Okay, okay."

A smile broke through the clouds of her tears. "You'll love it here, Nate. It's only a little farther from the Institute."

"I don't want to live here."

She broke into sobs again. He'd seen her this way only a few times in his life, and it sucked. It was terrifying that she relied so heavily on him, but it seemed to be one of those crappy cards he'd been dealt. Just like his father, apparently.

191

He patted her shoulder. "I'll move back in this weekend."

"My sweet boy," she cried, standing up to bury her face against his chest. "You'll never leave me."

This was it. This was his life. He had no room for anything else but taking care of his mother.

Which left nothing for him and Becky. Swallowing his own tears, he rubbed her back and resigned himself to a life without Becky in it. He'd been kidding himself.

He couldn't play at happiness anymore.

Chapter 16

Becky walked by the bakery Wednesday afternoon on her way to the coffee shop, spotting her brother inside. It was almost three o'clock and she knew he'd be headed over to the coffee shop to finish out his work day. His usually-sunny disposition wasn't present this afternoon, though. When he sat down at the table he'd just wiped down, she knew something was bothering him. She entered the bakery, humming along with the five-note chime as she approached him.

"Hey, bro."

He looked up, his brown eyes sad. "Hey, Becky."

There wasn't anyone else in the place, and by the sounds coming from the kitchen she knew that Caro and her assistant Jane must be back there prepping for tomorrow.

"Dinner at mom's was nice last night. I thought you might have brought Ashlyn, though."

"No."

"She's not here today?"

"No. She was, but she had to leave early."

She plopped down next to him. "You two seem like you're getting somewhere?"

193

Tom screwed up his face and immediately looked about seven years old. "Getting somewhere?"

She folded her arms on the tabletop. "I only meant that you've been seeing a lot of her."

"Not as much as I'd like."

Becky arched a brow and his cheeks reddened.

"Not like that!" He looked around the bakery as if checking to make sure no one would hear them before facing her again. "Jeez, sis. I meant that she's been busy and I've been busy."

"I know. You're a lazy, two-job kind of guy," she teased.

Her brother nodded. "Plus there's this thing with her father."

"What thing?"

Tom frowned. "He's sick. Really sick I think, but she doesn't talk about him much."

Tom hadn't even been a teenager when their dad died, so she was certain that this was bringing up a lot of sad memories.

"Do you know…" She swallowed, her own grief swiftly coming to the surface even after all this time. "What's wrong with him?"

"I think it's cancer. Not his heart, like with dad."

She wouldn't presume to think that one was better than the other, but at least Ashlyn would have the chance to say goodbye to her father if he didn't get better.

"Are they saying it's terminal?"

Tom shrugged. "It's prostate, but that's not fatal all the time is it?"

"I don't think so."

He gave a slow nod. "I hope he's okay. For Ash's sake."

They both fell silent, each in their own heads for several minutes. She thought about dinner at the inn last night. Zach and Joy talking easily with their mom. Kidding around with Tom. Fielding probing questions from her big sister. The memories sent warmth covering Becky. She'd missed that, hanging with her family. Her self-imposed exile had little to do with Nate, though. She'd started to distance herself soon after she'd moved into her condo.

"Does Ashlyn have any brothers or sisters?"

"Nope. It's just her and her dad. Her mom died about five years ago."

"Well, that sucks." Becky reached over to cover Tom's hand with hers. "You're a good friend to her, Tom. You'll be an even better boyfriend."

He snorted. "If that ever happens. Probably never."

"Never say never, little bro."

Becky thought about her roundabout path to Nate and laughed a little. "Look at me and Nate. We dated back in high school and then, nothing."

"And now you're, what?" he asked. "Serious?"

"Jeez, you sound like Joy. I'm not at all sure about serious, but I seriously like him."

"Like me and Ashlyn."

She smiled at him. "Like you and Ashlyn."

Punching him lightly in the shoulder, she stood and left him to finish his work. She really wasn't sure about her and Nate, other than the fact that they were having a good time. Not bed-buddies, or anything like that. Genuinely having a good time.

Last night he'd come back from his mother's and knocked on her door to say good night. That had surprised her, since most nights they went to sleep together. Something was up, but she wasn't going to pry. He didn't talk to her much at work today either, but he wasn't really a chatty kind of guy. Something was bugging him, though.

Later that afternoon, while she was closing down her computer and making notes about tomorrow's appointments, Nate approached her desk.

"Hey, Becks."

She looked up, losing her smile as she saw the frown lines between his pretty eyes.

"What's up?"

"We need to talk."

Her breath caught. *Whoa.* Were there any more ominous words in the English language? He didn't *want* to talk. He *needed* to talk. *Crap.*

"O-okay." Her hands trembled a little as she finished up and grabbed her bag. "Where?"

He shrugged one of his broad shoulders. "Your place okay?"

This wasn't good. She could feel it. Her stomach churned and her head spun for a second, but she'd been feeling kind of iffy ever since dinner last night. Today, though? This feeling right now? That had nothing to do with her mother's chops.

"Sure." She stood, at a loss and trying to get on more sure footing. "Let's go."

"You two heading out?" Harmony asked as she came into the reception area.

Becky managed a smile for her friend. "Yep."

"Have a good one," Harmony said.

She could only nod in response as she and Nate walked silently toward where his truck was parked.

***

Nate felt sick to the pit of his stomach. He didn't want to have this conversation, but it was only fair to let Becky know the shitshow that was his life right now.

She climbed into the passenger side of his truck and he walked around the back. She hadn't ridden her bike to work today, in fact most days they rode in together. Add that to the list of things coming to an end after tonight.

"How was your day?" he asked, eager to break the silence.

She shot him a look and a small, fleeting smile. "Great. Good. Good day."

Her voice was stilted. He knew her body better than his own, and could tell by the way she held herself that she was bracing herself for whatever was coming. He supposed that was good. He'd had almost twenty-four hours to get used to the idea of never being with her again. He regretted that couldn't give her that dubious luxury.

They made their way down the hallway toward their respective condos. He would keep his for the time-being. Mrs. Barnes was counting on it and he'd have to pay if he was still able to live there, right?

Becky's keys jingled as she tried to unlock her door. Settling his hand over hers, her skin was so soft and warm beneath his, he helped her open it. She gave him a small nod of thanks and hurried over to her kitchen.

"I have a feeling we're going to need wine," she said as she took two glasses down from a cabinet.

"Maybe." He sat on one of the stools at her tall counter. "I'll leave that up to you."

That stilled her. Leaving the glasses on the back counter, she crossed over to him.

"Can you just tell me what's wrong, Bugs? The suspense is killing me."

He nodded. "We can't see each other anymore."

She blinked rapidly. "What? Why, exactly?"

"Because of me, Becks."

He stood and began to pace, fighting the nausea as he tried to find the right words to end the only perfect thing he'd ever found.

"I have to take care of my mother. She needs me, and it's my job to look after her."

She scoffed aloud, causing him to turn back to her.

"What?" he asked her.

"It's your job?"

He raked a hand through his hair. "You don't know how it is. You had a mom and a dad growing up. I was the only one who was ever there for her."

"So what does that have to do with us?"

"Us? What, exactly, do you mean by us?"

She pulled back, her face pale. "I see."

He cursed softly. "I didn't mean that."

As he watched, the color came back into her cheeks. Her warm brown eyes took on a flinty glare.

"Hey, we were just hanging out," she said. "Hooking up. Fooling around."

Anger simmered in his sore belly now. "That's bullshit."

"Then you tell me what we were, Nate." She crossed her arms. "It's been almost two months since we started this…whatever it is. If you want to say it's over, you have to say what's over."

"That's ridiculous."

"No. A man who hides behind his mother? That's ridiculous."

He winced. Her arrow hit its mark, and he bit back further argument. "Fine. Call it what you want. I guess we're done either way."

The expression on her face, eyes rounded and mouth an O, said it all. "You guess?"

"Becky, this thing we had. Us, you called it. It's the closest I ever got to something real."

Her eyes were shiny now. "Something real?"

"Yeah." He huffed out a breath. "But it wasn't, was it? It was just a way to spend time."

He knew he hurt her with his words, but he'd rather have her mad at him than sad for what they'd lost.

"Spending time? Wasting time, you mean." She shook her head, a short laugh with zero humor in it coming from her lips. "And I thought it was bad when Kent was cheating on me. This? This is much worse."

He clenched his fists, attempting to keep from grabbing her. He wanted to hold her. To kiss her. To have her again. He craved her like he had ten years ago. Like he still did since the first time he'd seen her again.

"Becks."

She held up a hand, her face turned from him. "Don't even."

He stood there, rooted to the floor. "I don't know what to say."

"Say goodbye, Nate. That's more than you did ten years ago."

Another jab that hit its mark. Straight to his gut. He reached for her and pulled her close. He breathed her in, that sweet hot scent that would always be Becks.

"Can I kiss you one last time?" he asked, his mouth close to hers.

She was shaking now, but her body curved against his. "Bugs."

There was need in her voice. They might be over but they could have one more night together. He kissed her, hard and hot and perfect. She kissed him back, moaning as she wrapped her arms around his neck. He cupped her butt, pulling her up tight against him. His pulse pounded and heat flashed over him.

He tugged her shirt out of her pants, running his hands over the smooth skin on her back. Their tongues tangled and their breathing was harsh. Then she pulled away.

"No." She placed a hand in the center of his chest, stroking slightly before pushing at him. "No way."

He shook his head, still lost in the sensual haze that surrounded them. "What?"

"We're not going to do this, Nate. One last bang before we end this?"

"That's not what I wanted."

"Like fun, it's not." She gave herself a shake and wrapped her arms around her waist. "I can't do this. Love you and then say goodbye."

His pulse kicked. "Love?"

Her face held sadness he could hardly face.

"I could have loved you, you know," she said. "I was halfway there when you walked into the Institute all those weeks ago."

Shit. "Becks, please."

203

She closed her eyes, her long lashes brushing her cheeks. "Go, Nate."

His body was still hard, his mouth still filled with the taste of her. "I'm sorry," he muttered, unable to say anything else at that second.

She lifted her chin and faced him again. "Just go."

His head down, he let himself out of her place and crossed the hall to his own. For now, at least.

Sinking into his very nice couch, he buried his face in his hands. The tears were hot and stung when he finally let them out. He figured he could congratulate himself for how cool he'd played it at Becky's.

She had no idea that he was half in love with her, too.

Chapter 17

Becky rolled onto her side, rubbing the grit from her eyes. She'd slept like crap, which shouldn't be a big surprise. Nate's "talk" last night had seriously screwed with her equilibrium. Why she was nauseated, though? She had no clue.

After sending a text to Dr. Robbins to let him know she'd be a little bit late, a first in her memory, she got into the shower. Still dragging, she dressed in her perkiest Institute uniform and pulled her damp hair into a ponytail. Then it hit her. Nate wouldn't be driving her to work this morning. That was done. She tugged the ponytail holder out of her hair and placed it over her wrist. Like every other morning before Nate had come back into her life.

"Why did he have to come back?" she muttered.

She found one last strawberry shortie in the fridge and gobbled it up with a cup of coffee for a chaser. Not the best breakfast, but she was entitled wasn't she?

"No wallowing," she told herself. "It's not a good look."

There was no sign of Nate in the hallway, but there wouldn't be. He was as punctual as she normally was, so he was long gone. If he'd even spent the night in his place last night.

What was up with him? Letting his mother run his life? Donna liked Becky. That was clear. She was just dependent on her son and Nate willingly placed himself in the role of her protector. That was something Donna couldn't change, if he couldn't.

By the time she arrived at the Institute, miraculously only ten minutes late, there were three people in the reception area. They were thumbing through one of several nature magazines from the glass and rattan tables or the literature pamphlets set in the rack against one wall.

"Good morning," she said, a little out of breath.

Two of them, forty-ish women she recognized as long-time residents Marge and Marigold Atkins, greeted her in unison. The third one, an older man with sandy brown hair and blue eyes, smiled. There was something familiar about him, but she didn't think she'd ever met him before.

Becky skirted behind her desk and pulled up the day's schedule. "You're all here for an eco-tour, right?"

"Yes," the man said. "My daughter said I have to get back to nature. It would be good for my health."

She glanced at his face again, and noticed that he was a little pale despite his rugged appearance.

"Dave's daughter is right," Marge said in her usual, no-nonsense tone of voice.

She was the sturdier of the two sisters, compared to Marigold's willowy frame. The outward differences didn't end there, either. Marge kept her steel gray hair cropped short while Marigold kept her gray-streaked brown hair in a long, thick braid. Marge tended to dress in jeans or khakis, and today wore a sleeveless top with work boots. Marigold wore one of her usual broomstick skirts over her own half boots, paired with a flowy top embellished with mirrored sequins.

Becky had interacted with them many times over her years at the Institute, and she'd have a tough time finding any two residents more committed to nature in general and Cypress Corners in particular.

"You'll enjoy the tour." Becky checked the appointment and smiled at the man. "Mr. McCall."

He smiled, and she returned the expression. "Marge and Marigold will be perfect companions."

The sisters smiled at the well-deserved compliment, and began to chatter when Ty Walsh stepped inside.

"Ladies, how nice to see you both again." Ty waved at Becky. "Good morning."

"Good morning," Becky said. "You have a newbie today, Ty. This is Mr. McCall."

The men shook hands.

"Pleasure to meet you, Mr. McCall."

"Please, call me Dave."

"Dave it is." Ty looked at Becky once more. "Just three this morning, Becky?"

"Yes."

Ty nodded and rubbed his hands together. "Then lets get started. We'll head out in the Gator."

As he led the three of them out toward the back where the all-terrain vehicles were parked, Becky sat back down and tried to set aside the feeling that she'd be playing catchup all morning.

She knew when Nate stepped into her space, even without looking up. She could feel him, his heat and his presence, before his scent struck her.

"Good morning," he said, his voice flat.

She mumbled something, she wasn't quite sure what, and focused on her desktop. Keeping her expression even, she continued to look up the director's appointments and grabbed another stack of completed interest cards from visitors to their booth at the festival. That felt like a lifetime ago, working closely with Nate and watching him with the kids.

He left then, and she knew from handling his appointments as well that he had a meeting with Rick Chapman over at the Sales Center this morning. Once the doors whooshed shut behind him, she could breathe a little easier.

"That wasn't so hard," she murmured.

"What wasn't so hard?" Harmony asked.

Becky looked up at her friend and, when she opened her mouth to dismiss any potential discussion, she burst into tears.

Harmony gasped and hurried over to her. "Oh my, what's wrong?"

Becky just kept crying, unable to catch her breath. "I don't know why I'm crying," she rushed out. "It's stupid, that's all."

"What's stupid?"

Sniffling, Becky attempted to rein in her ridiculous outburst. "I'm sorry, Harmony. I don't know what's wrong with me. I didn't sleep well last night."

That's not all that happened last night, but she wasn't going to open that particular can of worms. Nate could probably recite those worms' species and genus, given the chance.

Giving herself a mental shake, she shoved him out of her mind. "I'm just tired, I guess."

Harmony narrowed her eyes. "There's something else, Becky. You know you can talk to me."

"Yes, but there's nothing to talk about."

Harmony straightened, crossing her arms. "Then it's just a coincidence that Nate is dragging himself around this morning, too?"

"He is?" she nodded. "Good for him."

"What happened between you two?"

"Nothing." She began to stack the interest cards on her desk, a little forcefully and bending the corners of a few of them. "Nothing that matters, anyway."

"That's telling, but I won't press you." She touched Becky's shoulder. "You do look a little pale, though. Did you eat breakfast this morning?"

"I had something."

"Not enough, I'd guess."

Becky shrugged. Harmony clapped her hands together. "Then let's do lunch together today. We'll make it an early one."

"I was late coming in as it is, Harmony."

"Pfft, ten lousy minutes. Who's counting?"

"Me, and Dr. Robbins."

"The doc wouldn't worry about you, Becky. He has no reason to."

"That's nice of you to say."

"Wow, you really are down today. It's so not like you."

"I'll see you for lunch."

"At eleven. I don't know why, but I've been starving lately."

"Maybe you're having a baby?"

Harmony laughed, and then sobered a little. "Maybe so."

Becky gaped. "You're going to have another baby?"

She waved a hand. "I don't think so, but it's a possibility."

"Nick is what, seven now?"

"Yep. I'm too old to have another baby anyway."

"Old? Who are you kidding? Plus, you look as young as Ashlyn."

"I doubt that, but thanks. Speaking of Ashlyn, did you know that was her father?"

"Who?"

"The guy taking the tour with the Atkins sisters."

"That makes sense. I thought he looked familiar."

She didn't share with Harmony what Tom had told her about the man's health, though. She hoped that getting back to nature would be good for him.

"Okay, so eleven?" Harmony asked.

Becky gave Harmony a salute, and her friend went down the hall to her office. Now if only Nate would stay out of her sight for the foreseeable future, maybe she could get through today and tomorrow.

Then she would have the whole, lonely weekend to herself to wallow in misery.

***

"What kind of bug crawled up your butt, Nate the Great?"

Nate lifted his brows as he eyed Oliver from across the breakroom table. "Huh?"

"You're dragging about two inches off the ground, buddy. What's wrong?"

"Nothing." *Everything.* "Just thinking about the meeting."

"You met with Rick Chapman. He's intense, but I've never known anyone to come out of his office looking as hangdog as you do right now."

"I'm fine," he bit out.

Oliver held up his hands. "Okay, my bad. Forget I said anything."

Nate nodded. "Sorry I snapped at you."

"No worries." Oliver fussed over his choice of coffee pod as he hummed to himself. "Want me to make you a cup?"

"No, thanks." He held up the bottle of water he'd grabbed from the fridge. "I'm set."

Zach Harris popped his head into the breakroom. "Hey, Nate. Lettie said she'd seen you come in here."

"Lettie is never wrong," Oliver quipped.

"What do you need?"

"We were talking the other night over at the inn, and Becky said you might like to help me out with something."

Knives seemed to stab at him at the mention of her

name, but he managed to meet Zach's gaze directly. "Help you out with what?"

"I'm going to be coaching the little guys soon. Summer sessions to get them ready for the fall. Like a farm team."

"Farm team." Like his father. "How little?"

"Five to seven, I'm guessing. It's just that I've been so busy out at the stables, finding the time to coach every session is getting tough."

Nate thought for a second, and then nodded again. "I'd love to help you out. How often would you need me?"

"They have the general coaches and assistants, mostly through the community school. They need specialties, man. Pitching. Catching. Something to focus the kids on those fundamentals."

Nate found a smile. "I take it you coach pitching?"

"Damn right. So will you, if you can swing it."

"Swing it!" Oliver laughed. "Good one, Zach."

Zach and Nate shared an eye roll. Zach drew out his phone. "Give me your number. I'll text you and you'll have mine."

Nate did so. "Let me know where and when. It'll give me something to do."

214

"Something to do?" Zach punched in the numbers and then pocketed his phone. "You're in Cypress, man. There's always something to do."

Nate dipped his head to acknowledge his statement.

Zach patted his shoulder. "I'll be in touch."

"Cool," Nate said.

"You're going to coach?" Oliver asked. "That *is* cool. Todd's store is supplying the uniforms and equipment for the little guys."

"Do they have sponsors?"

Oliver screwed up his face. "Not sure. Ask Zach. Or get with Todd, maybe?"

"I'll ask Zach and take it from there."

Oliver tilted his head to the side. "You know, there's a spark in those pretty eyes of yours Nate the Great. It's nice to see."

"I could use the distraction, but that's all I'll say."

Oliver gave him a small smile. "All right, then." He glanced at his phone. "Gotta run. I have an appointment in five."

He was gone from the breakroom and Nate was left to stew. He was delaying his return to the Institute, and felt like

215

the coward he was. Focusing on this new thing with Zach would be good, but he'd be working closely with Becky's sister's guy. He seemed pretty easygoing, but what would happen once they all found out what a pussy Nate was? What a dick he'd been to Becky?

He finished his water and tossed the bottle in the recycling container before finally dragging himself back to the Institute.

"Nate, how is your mother doing?" Sharon Walsh asked him before he stepped out of the Sales Center.

Nate took one look at the woman and saw that she knew about Chip and how he'd hurt his mother.

"She's not good, Mrs. Walsh."

"You're a good son, but you shouldn't take everything on yourself."

"I don't know about that."

Her mouth set for a minute before she gave a slight nod. "Forgive me for saying so, but you need to live your own life too."

His stomach churned again. "Thanks."

His tone was short and Sharon's lips thinned. "Tell your mother hello, and to call me?"

"Will do."

When he got back to the Institute he kept his head down. It turned out he didn't need to, since Becky's chair was vacant. Returning to his office, he settled behind his desk. His calendar app dinged, and his upcoming appointments were laid out for him. Becky was great at her job, and she wouldn't be one to screw him over. Even if he deserved it.

Mrs. Walsh said he needed to live his own life.

"Yeah, right."

He'd lived his own life, for a while. He wasn't thinking about his disaster of a relationship with Laura. That was destined to fail from the start. His heart hadn't been in it. That was for sure. No, it was his connection to Becky, that remarkable reacquaintance that had become so much more in so short a time.

"And now it's over."

Completely at his doing, but it was what it was. Until his mother could truly face life without him to hold her up, he would be there for her.

His own so-called life be damned.

Chapter 18

Becky sat in the tavern, picking at her burger. She'd wanted the thing when she'd ordered it, ravenous for red meat. Then it came, and looking at its pink inner belly she'd nearly vomited.

"Sis, you okay?" Joy asked.

In the week since her breakup with Nate, she'd hardly been okay.

"Sure. I think I'm just coming down with something."

Joy eyed her. "You do look a little peaked. What did you eat for lunch?"

"You sound like Mom. I had a container of yogurt and some animal crackers."

Joy chuckled. "What, no snack pack? That's a lunch a little kid would have."

"That's all I wanted."

"How long have you been feeling sick?"

"I'm not sick," Becky said. "I just don't... I guess I don't want a burger after all."

"Maybe you need a beer," Zach said, holding up his long-neck. "My treat."

"Thanks, but no thanks," Becky said. "The thought of

having one makes me want to…never mind."

Zach's eyes rounded. "Nuff said."

Joy gave him a small smile. "Would you mind if I talked to my sister alone for a minute?"

"Sure." He kissed Joy and stood. "I'll head over to the bar. Chase said he might be in tonight."

Zach left to see if his brother was at the bar, and Becky knew she would have to face Joy's questions head on.

"Tell me, Becky." Her brows scrunched together. "Tell me what happened between you and Nate."

"We broke up. Actually, he broke up with me."

Joy's lip curled. "That rat bastard."

"I appreciate the support, but it is what it is."

"Ugh, I hate that saying. You hate that saying, too. Admit it."

"I do." Her eyes pricked and she swallowed thickly. "I was falling for him, Joy. For everything about him. He wasn't falling, though. He was just wasting time."

Joy sucked in a breath. "Did he tell you that?"

Becky shook her head. "No, but it's true. What were we, exactly? Just two idiots trying to recapture something we never really had in the first place."

"That's bull, and you know it."

"Maybe. Either way, it sucks to be me."

"A Rollins doesn't wallow."

"One of dad's sayings." Becky smiled. "I'd forgotten that one."

"It's as true today as the day he said it to me. I think I was bummed out about missing a word in the spelling bee."

"And I was bummed out that I hadn't made the cheerleading squad."

"So what does a Rollins do?" Joy asked.

Becky blinked. "A Rollins looks for the silver lining. Sadly, no silver lining here that I can see."

"True, you're alone." At Becky's huff Joy held up a hand. "For the time-being. I can't see the two of you staying apart for very long."

"He won't be back."

"He's not seeing somebody else, is he? Behind your back?"

"No, he's not."

"That's something, at least."

"Cold comfort, but yeah."

"Come on, sis." Joy stood. "Let's get out of here. We'll

go by the coffee shop where we can talk in peace."

"What about dinner?"

"I'll tell Zach to have it wrapped to go. I can meet up with him later."

"Okay." Becky stood, and the floor seemed to tilt beneath her. Grabbing on to the table, she tried to steady herself but that was wobbling too. "God."

"Becky!" Joy wrapped an arm around her shoulders. "What's wrong?"

"I don't know."

Joy tugged her out of the tavern toward the ladies room. "Let's go splash some water on your face."

She spoke to Zach, in that shorthand they seemed to have. He nodded and patted Becky's arm before heading back to their table.

Once in the ladies room, Becky stared at her ghostly complexion. "Jeez, I can count every freckle."

"You look like crap," Joy said. "Want to tell me now, what's wrong?"

"I guess this breakup hit me harder than I thought it would."

"How long has it been?"

"About a week or so."

Joy shook her head. "No. How long since your last period?"

"What?" Becky's pulse tripped. "You're crazy."

"You're nauseated, Becky. You're hungry and then you can't eat. Tell me I'm wrong."

"Of course you're wrong." Something niggled at the back of her mind. Something that had happened just over a month before. Her breath caught. "No."

"No, what."

"No, this can't be happening."

"You're late, aren't you."

Becky nodded. "And there was this one time we didn't use… Oh, but I can't get pregnant from just one time."

Joy nodded sagely. "Says every pregnant high school girl since the dawn of time."

Becky covered her face with her hands. "I can't be pregnant. Is the market still open?"

Joy glanced at her phone. "Yep. I'll go grab a test and come right back."

Becky breathed in slowly through her nose and leaned back against the counter. Could she be pregnant? That would just be the icing on the cake, wouldn't it? Having a baby with a guy who didn't want to be with her? She just wouldn't tell him.

"Don't borrow trouble," she murmured.

There was no reason to think she got pregnant from the one time Nate didn't use a condom. That night he'd been so passionate, so eager to be together, that he'd let go of the control he normally clung to like a life raft. She'd brushed it off, too. It was too much to consider that one night would have these kinds of consequences.

"I'm just coming down with the flu or something." She splashed more water on her face, feeling a little bit better as she chose to believe that explanation. "That's all."

But that wasn't all. Her sister came back with a pregnancy test and, in just under two minutes, she was staring at the proof that she'd tried to ignore.

She was pregnant with Nate's child.

"What are you going to do?" her sister whispered.

Becky waved the plastic tell-all stick in the air before tossing it into the trashcan. "I'm going to have a baby."

A smile teased her lips and she felt a surge of happiness at this major screw up. "I'm going to have a baby!"

She laughed and threw her arms around her sister, who hugged her back.

"Yeah, you are!" Joy sounded happy, too.

They both pulled back to stare at each other.

"Don't tell Mom," they said at the same time.

Then they hugged again.

She'd have to deal with all of it, telling Nate and her family, eventually. Tonight, though? Tonight she would focus on the fact that she was having a baby she hadn't planned but wanted fiercely.

The rest would have to work itself out.

***

Nate stood with Nick Chapman, teaching him the proper stance on the mound. The kid was a natural, and took his direction well. Max Brady stood at home plate, and Noah and Jessie's little boy looked determined as he tried to hit the balls Zach was softly lobbing to him. This was Nate's third week helping out with the kids, and he found it was a great escape from the mess that was his life right now.

He felt as trapped as a fly in a spiny orb weaver's web. His mother was still no better since her breakup with Chip, but who was he to judge? He wasn't doing very well without

Becky, was he? And he'd made that mess all by himself.

The evening was still very warm, but there was a breeze. The kids didn't seem to be bothered by it, and the staff made sure that there was plenty of sports drink and that they took frequent breaks.

"Okay, go rest your arm," he told Nick. "Grab yourself a drink from the cooler."

Nick did as he was told, and Nate took a second to look over the kids. They were tough for little guys, and this was much more fun than he'd originally thought it would be. Zach was becoming a good buddy, too. The guy had mentioned Becky only once, and that was at the very beginning. Now that they'd worked together several times, things were nice and easy between them. There was a little bit of friendly rivalry, but that only made this whole experience better for Nate. Baseball rivalry, he could handle. Jokes and jabs were easy to deal with. He caught sight of red hair and his heart sped up for a second before he realized it was Tom, Becky's brother.

"Hey, Zach." He loped on over to join them. "Joy said you guys could use another grownup."

"You're a grownup now?" Zach teased.

"Shut up," Tom said without anger. "Hey, Nate."

There is was. That hesitancy. Tom was Becky's little brother, but Nate suspected he could be as protective as any big one.

"How's it going, Tom?" Nate asked.

Tom shrugged in answer. Before long, he was running around with the kids and getting into it. Nate let Tom's brushoff go, and almost before he realized it the two-hour session was over.

"Come on, kids!" the coach called from over by the cooler.

The little boys flocked to the big guy and Zach came to stand next to Nate.

"So how's everything with you?" he asked Nate.

"Fine," he answered. "A little chilly."

"Look, man. I'm not going to pry. Joy only told me a little bit about your breakup and I'm not one to judge. I've only had one serious relationship in my life and, thankfully, I've still got her."

"Joy is your only serious relationship?"

Zach smiled. "Yep. She's the one for me. That's it. End of story."

Nate fell silent. He'd thought the same thing about Becky. He'd even hoped for some kind of future, not they'd ever talked about it. It had all been very "in the here and now." They'd just taken things as they were. He missed her, and not just the sexy stuff.

"I don't think I'll ever have that," he admitted on a breath.

"Maybe you won't. Not if you were dumb enough to let Becky get away."

Nate shot him a look. "I thought you weren't going to pry."

"I'm not prying, just stating an fact. Those Rollins girls, they get under you skin. Real quick."

Nate couldn't argue with that. "It's killing me to see her every day."

"She's probably got that going on to, although she might look a little peaked because she's been sick."

Nate's pulse tripped. "She's sick?"

Zach's eyes rounded. "Nothing serious, I don't think."

"Still, I'm sorry she's sick."

Zach gave a quick nod. Nate thought for a second. Becky had looked pale and a little tired over the past couple of weeks. Guilt twisted the knife already deep in his gut.

"Joy doesn't seem too worried, though," Zach added. "So it can't be serious."

"It's serious," Tom cut in as he joined them. "Don't sugarcoat it for this dick."

"Tom," Zach said in obvious warning.

"What's going on?" Nate asked.

Tom eyed him, then his brows rose. "You don't know, do you? This isn't an act."

"An act?" Nate turned to Zach. "What's he talking about?"

Zach stared at him, a look of compassion stamped on his face. "Man, it's not my place."

Tom cursed, and that shocked Nate more than the angry expression on his face. He'd never heard him swear before.

"It's sure as hell your place," Tom said, shoving Nate in the chest.

"What the hell?" Nate straightened. "Spit it out, Tom."

"She's pregnant, you son-of-a-bitch."

Nate felt the blood drain from his face as he clenched his fists. "What?" he managed to ask.

"Tom, why did you do that?" Zach asked. "Becky asked

us not to say anything."

"Why?" Nate murmured.

"He deserves to know what he did, leaving her like that," Tom said.

"She's pregnant?" Nate stared hard at Zach until the other guy nodded.

"Yeah," Zach said.

Nate's chest felt tight and he thought for a second he might pass out. "She's pregnant," he said again.

"Yeah, she is," Tom said. "And you're going to stay the hell away from her."

"Tom," Zach said. "That's not for us to say."

"It sure as hell is. First he dumps her and now this?"

"I didn't…" Nate could hardly catch his breath. "It wasn't like that."

"You know what, Nate? I don't care." He got up in Nate's face. "I only care about my sister, and you're not going to hurt her again."

"I would never hurt her," Nate said.

"Not on my watch, you're not." He stepped back. "You're going to stay away from her."

Zach pulled on Tom's arm. "Come on, bro. It's time to

get home. Nate, I'll see you around."

Nate gave a shaky nod and closed his eyes. By the time the world stopped spinning around him, everyone was gone from the park. It was past sunset, and the shadows from the trees overhead were long under the glare from the streetlights as he walked to his truck. Becky was pregnant.

She didn't want to be around him. Hell, she hadn't even wanted him to know. He did know, and he was going to talk to her whether she liked it or not. He might not know what the hell he was going to do now, but he knew one thing.

His kid wasn't going to grow up without its father.

Chapter 19

Becky sipped an iced herbal tea in the coffee shop courtyard, grateful that her nausea tended to restrict itself to the mornings. It was a pretty Saturday afternoon, and she had no claims on her time today. She'd told her mother about the baby at Tuesday's family dinner, and Tom too. Her little brother was not happy with Nate. The words "string him up by his balls" were heard, despite the shock on her mother's face at that outburst.

Becky had gone to the doctor on the square, and he'd confirmed what the plastic stick had shown that night in the tavern's bathroom. She was having a baby. Nate's baby. And, aside for her family, she was alone. A hand settled over her still-flat tummy. Not entirely alone.

"Look at you," Lettie said as she joined her. "Pretty as a sunny Saturday afternoon in July."

"Spot on as always," Becky teased. "What are you doing away from your usual spot?"

"Oh, I needed to stretch my legs." She leaned on the table. "Besides, you didn't seem to be inclined to come over and join me."

"I would have." Becky tipped her face up to the sun

peeping through the dappled shade of a tall sycamore tree. "Just wanted a few minutes to myself."

"On the crowded square in the middle of Cypress Corners?"

Becky glanced around and saw lots of people strolling by the shops and even riding surrey bikes. "I take my solitude where I can find it."

"Oh, pooh," Lettie said. "Solitude is for hermits and old maids."

Becky laughed and eyed the outrageous widow. "Lettie, you never cease to surprise me."

Lettie nodded, the wide brim of her straw sunhat flapping. "Then I've done my job. Living up to my reputation, such as it is."

Becky took another sip of her tea and straightened. "I could go for some of those strawberry shorties. If I ducked into the bakery, would you want me to get you one?"

"That would be lovely dear, but you don't have to do that."

Becky snapped her fingers. "You know what? Tom is working there right now. I bet if I asked him he'd bring some over."

"Curbside service?" Lettie smiled. "Why would your brother do that?"

Becky had been touched, and a little surprised, by Tom's reaction to her announcement on Tuesday night. She loved him for it, and he loved her just as much.

"It's worth a try," was all she'd say.

She drew out her phone and texted him. Less than five minutes later, he stood at her table with a bright green bag from Sweet Escape in one of his big hands.

"Strawberry shorties," he said, handing her the bag.

Becky opened the bag and breathed in the sweet, fresh scent. "Mmm, these are so good."

"I have something to tell you, sis."

She took a bite, letting the icing melt on her tongue. "Shoot," she mumbled around a mouthful of pastry.

Tom looked pointedly at Lettie, and then back at her. "It's about what you said Tuesday night."

"And?" she asked him.

"I said something."

Becky sat up straight again. "Tom, what did you do?"

Lettie crossed her arms. "Yes, dear boy. What did you do?"

233

Becky shot her a look. "Lettie, what do you mean?" She lowered her voice. "Do you know?"

Lettie smiled and leaned closer. "Honey, I do. But that is one bit of gossip I would never share."

Becky read the sincerity in the woman's kind eyes, and nodded her thanks.

"I said something," Tom said again.

"Tom, what?" It hit her then. "No."

He nodded. "Yeah. I'm sorry."

"Tom, you didn't!"

"He did," Nate said from somewhere behind her.

She turned her head and gaped at him. Nate, who with very few exceptions hadn't said two words to her since that awful night. Nate, who was glaring at her. Glaring? How dare he?

"Nate," she said.

"We need to talk."

That did it. She stood.

"We most definitely do not." She grabbed up her bakery bag and tea and went to walk past him. He grasped her arm and she stopped to stare down at his hand. "Let me go."

"Becks, please."

"Becks?" It was her turn to glare at him. "Not here. Not now."

"Let her go, man." Tom got up in Nate's face. "Don't make me finish what I started last night."

Nate dropped his hand from her.

"Last night?" Lettie asked. "Ah. Baseball practice."

Becky stared at her. Did the woman know everything?

"I'm going home, Nate," she said. "I don't care where you go."

"I have a few ideas," Tom said.

Oh, her little brother was a fierce protector. Who knew?

"Thanks, Tom," she said. "Don't sweat it."

"Please let me talk to you," Nate said.

His voice was as rich as she remembered. His scent as strong and his eyes as pretty. She couldn't afford to let down her guard, though. Not after the cold way he had shoved her aside like she had never even mattered.

"I'm going home," she said again.

Her Prius was parked at the curb, since she didn't trust herself to ride her bike over the last couple of weeks. Not with the nausea and dizziness that was always a possibility. She ignored Nate's gaze, along with what felt like the stares of everybody else on the square, and got into her car for the short ride home.

Thankfully the tears waited until she stepped into her condo, hot and angry tears she couldn't hold in any longer. Nate knew about the baby, and he needed to talk. Again.

A knock came at her door, and she knew who it was. How dare he? She went to the door and opened it, staring up at him.

"I should have let my brother punch you."

***

Nate could see that anger and hurt in her eyes again. He had to talk to her, though. There was a baby on the way, his baby, and he had to tell her where they stood.

"Becks, please."

She stepped back, pulling the door open wider. "Come in, Bugs."

The nickname, said without any apparent affection this time, cut him. He stepped inside and waited for her to shut the door.

"I had to see you."

"No, Nate. You need to talk."

"What?"

"Yet again, you need to talk." She crossed her arms. "So, talk."

His tongue felt about two sizes too big in his mouth, like it had been stung by forty wasps. This was too important to let his nervousness win out, though. This was their kid they were talking about.

"You're pregnant."

"I know."

He took a short breath. "I mean, I know that you're pregnant."

"Tom spilled the beans. He confessed right before you showed up."

Nate hadn't overheard much of their discussion as he'd walked up to the coffee shop but, by the guilt stamped on Tom's face, had guessed what it was about.

"Why didn't you tell me?"

"Why would I tell you?"

"What?"

"What is it to you? We aren't together anymore."

"I want to be."

She gaped at him. "Excuse me?"

"I want us to get back together."

237

"Suddenly you have room in your life for, what did you call it? Almost something real?"

"You're having my baby."

"We've established that."

"Then why are we arguing?"

"We're not arguing, Nate. You want us to get back together and that's not going to happen."

Acute frustration bit at him. "Look, I'm not going to let my kid grow up without knowing his father."

"Is that what this is about? Don't worry. I'll tell the baby who you are."

He growled. "That's not what I meant."

"Then tell me. What do you mean?"

"I want us to be together, Becks. For good."

"Ha. Because I'm pregnant? You've got to be kidding."

"Becky, please."

"No. I wasn't enough for you before. Now I suddenly am? Nope. Not going to happen."

He grabbed her like he had in the courtyard, pulling her closer this time. "Becky, this is our baby. We should be together."

She pulled out of his grasp and stood straight and stiff.

"Nate, this is our baby. That's undeniable. We, however, will not be together."

He was completely at a loss. "Why not?"

"Because you don't…"

The expression on her face made him stop short. Her color was high and her eyes wide.

"What?"

"Never mind." She slowly shook her head. "Go home, Nate."

His throat tightened. Maybe he had been stung. Maybe he'd asphyxiate and this would all be over. He'd never be that lucky, though.

"Becks, what we have…"

She arched one brow and, if it wasn't for the tears he could see clinging to her lashes, he would think she really was done with him. With them.

"I won't let this baby ever think they're not enough," she finally said.

"And I would?"

"You tell me? Seems to me that you like to keep things easy. You prefer a nice, smooth surface with no ripples. That's not a real life, Nate. And this baby? This baby is going to have a real life."

He wanted to grab her and shake her, to kiss her and have her again. To make her see that he meant this. He knew he had to prove they would be better together than apart, for the sake of their child. He also knew when it was time to step off the mound and take the loss.

"This isn't over, Becks."

She said nothing as he turned and let himself out. He stood in front of the door to his condo, still his by rental payments if not occupancy. If he lived across the hallway from her, she couldn't ignore him. Sure, they worked at the same place but he wasn't going to bring drama to the Institute. She had a prior claim on the place and everybody there and, despite how friendly and welcoming everyone had been, he was still the new guy.

There was nothing else to do. He had to talk to his mom.

"God, this is a mess," he grumbled.

Filled with irritation and frustration both, he stalked off to his truck to drive back to his mother's house. When he got there, she was bustling around the kitchen and singing a song he vaguely recognized.

"Hey, Mom."

She turned to him, a big smile on her face. Dread pooled in his belly. Something was up.

"Nate, honey! I'm so glad you're home."

He dropped his keys in the bowl on the counter. "What's up?"

"Nate, I've been thinking." She stopped and studied him. "What's wrong?"

"Nothing."

"Nate Bauer, you tell me what's wrong right now."

He sat at the kitchen table and shook his head. "It's a lot to deal with."

She joined him, touching his arm. "Do you think I can't handle it?"

"Mom, you have to admit that you're not very good at handling the tough stuff."

She pouted, and then shrugged. "If I didn't think you were right, I'd send you to your room."

That made him a smile a little. "This is the toughest mess I've ever been in."

"Worse than your breakup with Laura?"

He snorted. "What I had with Laura was barely a

relationship, so the breakup turned out to be no big deal."

"Then this has to do with Becky. I thought you two were fine."

His mouth dropped open. "You thought we were fine? Mom, we haven't been seeing each other since I moved in here."

She gasped. "What? You broke up with her to stay with me?"

"You begged me to move in," he bit out. "I thought that was what you wanted."

She stood and paced, one of her habits he'd inherited. "Nate, I never wanted you to sacrifice your happiness for me."

"Didn't you?" When she gasped again he held up both hands. "Never mind. What's done is done. Now Becky won't even speak to me."

"What's changed?"

"What do you mean?"

"Why are you trying to talk to her? Do you want to get back together?"

"I've missed her. It's been hell seeing her and not being with her. But I've really made a mess of it now."

She sat down again. "What happened?"

He took a breath. "She's pregnant."

The words hung in the air for a few seconds, before her mother cried out in joy.

"A baby! Oh Nate, that's wonderful!" She hugged him tight before sitting back down and swiping away her tears. Happy ones, he didn't have to guess. "You and Becky will have such a beautiful baby!"

He gave himself the luxury of a long minute to think about a kid with her fiery hair and his blue eyes. Or maybe his hair and her coffee-chocolate eyes. Would it have freckles? That would be amazing.

"Yeah, we will. But we won't be raising it together."

"Why not?"

"She doesn't want to be together just for the sake of the baby."

"Why would that be… Nate, what did you do?"

"I didn't do anything, not after our breakup anyway. She said that I don't love her. Or, I think that was what she was going to say."

"Oh." She nodded sagely. "She loves you, then."

"No, I don't think so." He stood now, walking around

the kitchen before leaning against one of the counters. "It doesn't matter. I don't want my kid to grow up never knowing his father."

She winced. "I deserve that. That's what I wanted to tell you, actually."

"Huh?"

"Your father, Nate. He's back in my life."

Chapter 20

Of all the things she could have said, that was the one Nate had never expected. He was glad for the counter at his back, because his knees threatened to buckle.

"What?"

"Your father, Nate. He's moved back down to Florida for good."

"What do you mean, for good?"

Her gaze slid to the tabletop and she played with the fringe on one of the placemats. "He's been coming down every so often."

"You've been seeing him. All this time."

"No!" Her head snapped up. "His wife passed away five years ago."

"You've been seeing him." It wasn't a question. "For five years."

"No," she said again. "Only when he would come down in the winter to visit his daughter. She lives here in Cypress, believe it or not."

"Why didn't you ever tell me? All those times over the past five years?"

"I didn't want to get your hopes up. He still had his

245

business up north, and we're both pretty set in our ways."

His mind boggled and he tried to grab onto something solid. "What's changed?" he asked, using her earlier words.

"He's been sick, but he's getting better."

"So, why tell me now?"

"Because he's been asking me about you."

"He knows I'm in Cypress?"

"He knows we both are. He has very little family, you see. Just a daughter a few years younger than you."

Things seemed to click into place. "The time you told me about, Mom. The time you tried to make it work. That was before his daughter was born?"

She nodded, her gaze misty. "She had health problems as a baby, Nate. He and his wife wanted to separate but they stayed together for their daughter." She smiled. "Your half-sister."

"Whoa." He shook his head. "This is a lot to take in."

"Will you meet with him?"

"No."

"No? Why not?"

"He's had twenty-eight years to reach out. I'll even be generous. Why didn't he tried to contact me after his wife died?"

"I don't know."

"And you never told me?" He started to pace again. "You were seeing my father on and off. My father! And I have a sister, too? This is too much."

"Just think about it, Nate. Take your time and think it through. You're so good at that, thinking about things."

He allowed that she was right with a dip of his head. "But this is a lot. And now with my baby on the way?"

"Don't you see? This baby is a blessing in so many ways! You'll get your Becky back and you'll be a real family."

"Real," he echoed. "She wants something real."

"Then give it to her."

"I don't think I can." His eyes stung and he swallowed hard. "I don't know how."

"That's my fault. All my fault."

"I'm a grown man, Mom. It's up to me to figure out how to be the man Becky and the baby need."

"You can do it, honey. Maybe you can be a little more receptive to your father?"

"I don't think so. It's too late."

"Nate, honey. It's never too late."

"You're seeing him again, aren't you?"

She nodded, her face beaming. "And it's for real this time."

"You've said that before," he pointed out gently.

"I know. But we've both changed, and he wants this to be for good."

"And what do you want?"

"I love him, Nate. I never stopped."

That made his chest tighten. "You've never said that."

"What do you mean?"

"You've been 'madly in love' or 'head over heels' but you've never said you love a guy before."

Her brow furrowed. "Hmm. You know, you're right. So will you meet with him?"

He raked a hand through his hair. "I don't know." He walked toward the back door. "I need to get some air."

"Okay, honey. You do have a lot to think about."

"Yeah." He turned back to her. "So what's this guy's name?"

She smiled again. "Dave McCall."

He filed that info away for now and headed out to St.

Cloud. He wouldn't go to the tavern and risk running into anybody he knew. From Cypress, anyway. He had a lot of thinking to do, and the End Zone would be perfect. Playing either a pickup game of pool or one of the old-fashioned pinball machines might be just what he needed right now.

About five minutes into his drive, their song came on the radio. Too late to apologize. Seemed about right, in his case. He changed stations and tightened his hands on the wheel.

The lot was packed, which was no surprise for a Saturday. He parked his big truck between two even bigger ones, and went inside. Ignoring the cozy booths, he strode right up to the bar. It was two people deep, but he had the advantage of height.

The bartender, a girl with dark hair and a lot of eyeliner, smiled up at him. "What will it be?" she rushed out.

"Summer Shandy, please," he said. "In a bottle."

She popped the top off of the seasonal beer and handed it to him. He dropped some bills on the bar. She took enough for the beer, so he handed her four more.

"And can I get some quarters?"

She gave him a couple of dollars' worth and pocketed

the rest. He took his beer and walked through the large opening toward the pool room.

The beer was cold in his hands, and he took a quick drink. The tables were packed, and there were clearly people waiting to shoot as well. He headed for the pinball machines and took another drink of his beer before setting it on the low ledge that ran around the perimeter of the game room.

He began to play, not thinking of anything but watching the steel ball careen around the playing surface. Striking it felt a lot like swinging a bat, and he'd always liked the sensation. He drained his beer between games and reached into his pocket for more quarters. A flash of red caught his eye, and he turned to see a pretty girl leaning on a pool cue. Her hair wasn't as fiery as Becky's, but more of a strawberry blond.

"Hey, I know you," she said. "You're Nate Bauer."

"Do I know you?"

She smiled. "No, but you know my husband. Jake Chapman."

"The Adventure Trails guy. Yes, I do."

"We're here with a few other people from Cypress. You should join us."

Alarm trilled through him. "No, thanks. I'm good."

"Okay, but you know a couple of them."

He followed where she pointed and saw that Ty and Cassie Walsh sat at a booth with Zach and Becky's sister.

"Ah, I better not. The Rollins family isn't too fond of me right now."

"But aren't you…?" She cut herself off and nodded. "Never mind. I heard you and Becky broke up."

"Yeah." He wondered what else she'd heard, but he sure as hell wasn't going to bring it up.

"Babe, our table just opened up." Jake Chapman stopped and smiled at Nate. "Hey, Nate."

"Hey."

"Come on, Claire," Jake said.

Claire looked like she wanted to say something more, but she turned away and followed her husband to a pool table near the back of the room.

Nate left the game room, bound for the bar. He was about to order another beer when that damn song came on the digital jukebox. Like the night he'd been here with Becky. Like the night that felt like ages ago.

Deciding against another drink, he left the End Zone and headed back to Cypress. He wasn't going back to his mother's house, though. Nope. He was going to move back in across the hall from Becky.

"Out of sight, out of mind," he said to himself. "Not this time."

He'd never figure this out if he was hiding at his mother's place like a baby. *Baby.* For the first time he allowed himself to smile at the thought of their child. It was coming, and it was time he stepped up to the plate.

***

"He moved back in?" Joy stared at Becky, her eyes round.

"Yep."

Joy smirked and held up her scone in salute.

"I have to hand it to him. Bugs has balls."

Becky had to laugh at that. They sat in the bakery on this sunny Saturday afternoon, since she'd found it a pretty safe place for her to hide from Nate. She was beginning to run out of places he didn't frequent.

"So how has it been, since he moved back?"

Becky nibbled on her strawberry shortie as she mulled over her sister's loaded question.

"It's only been a week, but I'm getting a little tired of

tiptoeing past his door."

"When you come in at the wee hours after a night of partying?" Joy teased.

Becky clicked her tongue. "In the morning, smarty pants. When he's all gallant and offers to drive me to work."

"You're not riding your bike?"

"No, not now. Probably not until after."

"After." Joy brightened. "You'll have a baby, after! You can get one of those baby seats and the kiddo can ride in front with a little helmet on."

It was an adorable picture to imagine, and she couldn't keep a smile from curving her lips. "That's some time from now, Joy."

"Still, I can totally see it."

Becky could too. The rest of the picture was much less clear to her. He'd asked her why they couldn't be together and she'd almost blurted out that he didn't love her! If she had? She would have had to admit that she loved him and that was so not happening.

"How are the Rollins sisters today?" Caro Graham sat down at their table with a soft groan. "I do care. Seriously, but I'm also beat."

"The baby?" Joy asked.

"Yes, Maddie's teething and she apparently thinks the whole household has to hear about it."

Maddie, named for the pastry Madeleine, was Caro and Eli's sweet miracle. Becky knew this, as much as she was counting her little oven-bun as one of her own.

"Is it very bad?" Becky asked.

Caro's brows rose. "It's bad for her, but it will pass."

"What do you do?" Becky pressed her.

"She has her chewy rings, and Daddy loves that he has an excuse to walk the floor with her again."

Joy smiled. "I remember you telling it a little differently back when Maddie had colic."

"Colic?" Becky's voice cracked.

"Easy, sis." Joy gave her a small smile.

Caro leaned closer. "Then it's true," she whispered.

Becky and Joy exchanged a look, and then Becky nodded. "It's true."

Caro's face lit. "Becky, that's wonderful news!"

"It is," Becky said.

Caro looked pointedly at Joy before facing Becky again. "Why do I think there's more than simple morning sickness causing those pale cheeks."

Becky brought her hands to her face. "I'm pale?"

"A Rollins can never be pale," Joy quipped. "We come packing freckles."

"Well played." Caro stood with a smile, leaning over to rest her hand on Becky's shoulder. "If you ever need to talk, I've been known to be up in the wee hours."

"Thanks, Caro."

Caro left them in relative privacy.

Becky shook her head. "Everybody knows, then."

"About the baby?" Joy shook her head. "Only a select few. I swore Zach to secrecy but our little brother has a big mouth. We've always known this."

"So Caro knows. Her assistant Jane, probably. Ashlyn?"

"I don't know about Jane but yeah, Ashlyn knows."

Becky looked over at Ashlyn standing behind the counter and intercepted the girl's sympathetic gaze.

"That's just great."

"Ashlyn won't tell anyone. She's got a lot on her plate right now."

"Her dad is sick," Becky said. "I know."

"Good news and bad, sis. It's all swimming around in

the fishbowl."

Becky folded her arms on the table. "Gotta love it."

"What does Mom have to say? You know, about the whole Nate situation."

Becky smiled when she recalled the very vivid statements her mother had used when she described what she wanted to do to her baby daddy. "Mom was Mom. Supportive and protective."

"Just what you needed, I'll bet."

"It was a little bit much, but I'm very lucky to have all of your support, Joy."

Joy stood and leaned over the table to give her a hug. "Always, little sister."

Ashlyn walked over to their table, tucking a loose strand of her wavy brown hair back behind one ear. "Hey, ladies."

Becky smiled up at her. "Hi, Ashlyn. How are you doing?"

"Okay. You know my dad moved down here for good."

"Tom told me," Joy said.

"I didn't know that," Becky said. "I bet he's happy to be closer to you."

"He is, and now that he's on the mend I'm really happy

about that too."

"You don't seem so happy right now," Becky said.

"It's just…" She looked around before leaning closer. "He's been seeing someone and I think it might be serious."

Becky knew the girl had lost her mom a few years ago, but it felt like there was something more than just dating going on.

"What's wrong?" Joy asked. "You don't like the woman?"

"No, she's sweet. Very sweet, actually. I just think there's a history there he's not sharing."

"History?" Becky asked. "Who is he seeing?"

"Donna Bauer."

That surprised Becky, but she was very happy the stink bug was no longer in the picture. The woman's son might be on Becky's list right now, but she couldn't deny that his mother was sweet.

"She's a very nice woman," she said.

Ashlyn nodded. "There's something my dad isn't telling me." Caro called to her and Ashlyn stood. "Gotta run."

"So Nate's mom is dating Ashlyn's dad," Joy observed. "That's just a coincidence."

"That must have been him, then," Becky said.

"Who?"

"This older man who took an eco-tour with the Atkins sisters last week. He said he was moving back down here to be close to family."

"Is he as nice as his daughter?"

"Yes. And worlds better than the stink bug Donna was dating before."

"Stink bug?" Joy snorted. "I'm thinking that was Nate's name for that guy."

"It was, but I'm not talking about him. Not thinking about him, either."

"Keep telling yourself that," Joy said.

Becky couldn't argue with her sister. Nate was never far from her mind. The door chimes rang and as she looked up, she began to doubt that she could stay away from him for very much longer. He looked so good, tall and broad with his hair slightly mussed. Her heart tripped and she dragged her gaze away.

"Wonderful," Becky grumbled.

Joy stood, gathering up their plates and napkins. "Come on, Becky."

Nate watched them, his blue gaze steady. As they passed him, she held her breath. Keeping her face turned from him, she stepped out onto the sidewalk in front of the bakery.

"Take a breath, sis," Joy said.

Becky did, willing her racing heart to slow. Just seeing him was enough to weaken her resolve.

"Would being together for the baby be such a bad thing?" Becky asked softly.

Her sister slowly shook her head. "That's your decision to make."

Becky couldn't do it. She couldn't be less than enough. Not again. No matter how hot Nate looked standing in that doorway.

Chapter 21

Nate pulled himself away from the door, forcing himself to focus on the girl wiping down the tables. He'd spotted Tom Rollins next door at the coffee shop, and taken it as a sign that the bakery was a safe zone. He hadn't expected to find Becky there, though. The low hum of need that was never far away had spiked, even after she'd left without a word. He had something else going on today, though. Someone he had to get to know at least a little bit. His half-sister.

He'd yet to have a conversation with Dave McCall, but his mother had informed him last night that Ashlyn was his daughter. So far, from what his mother told him at least, the man seemed to genuinely care for her, but as for his own relationship with the man? He'd yet to see him face to face, let alone get to know him to any degree. Tonight they were supposed to have dinner, just the three of them.

"Hey, Ashlyn," he began.

She stopped and straightened. "Nate, right?"

He nodded. "Yeah. Nate Bauer."

She frowned at him. "My boyfriend isn't very fond of you right now."

"Yeah, I know." Tom had every right to be pissed at

him, too.

She sniffed. "We're closing in a few."

"I know, I…" He waited a beat. "Your father is seeing my mother."

"I know that." A smile played around her mouth. "She's very sweet, your mother."

"She is."

"You can't have come here to talk about that."

"No."

"Well, I'm a little busy."

"Nate, what can I get you?" Caro Graham stepped over to them, a curious expression on her face.

"Um, what do you have left?"

"No more shorties." Her eyes narrowed. "You can guess why."

He rubbed the back of his neck. "I can. I wanted to take something over to my mom's."

"I have a few scones left, and a couple biscotti."

"I'll take whatever you've got."

"I'll go help Jane in the back," Ashlyn said to Caro.

She disappeared into the back without another word to Nate. He stepped over to the counter as Caro filled a box with the last of the treats from the bake case.

"I thought you were living with your mom," she said.

He flashed a quick smile. "No. I'm back in my own place."

She closed the box up tight and faced him. "How's that working out for you?"

"What do you mean?"

"You know." She took his credit card and began to ring him up. "Living across the hall from Becky again."

He mumbled something in answer and took the card and box from her. "Thanks."

She stood there for a beat, curiosity clear in her expression. Did she know about the baby? Eli hadn't said anything but, if Nate's time in Cypress had shown him anything, it was that the guys generally kept themselves out of the fish bowl if they could.

"Have a good night," he added.

"You too."

He couldn't stop himself from looking for Becky as he stepped back out onto the brick sidewalk. The coffee shop was still busy, and most of the tables in the courtyard were occupied. Lettie waved at him from her table and he returned

the gesture. He wouldn't head over there, though. She was
sure to ask about Becky and he was so twisted in knots over
their situation he was in no mood to trade information in the
guise of southern pleasantries.

It was a little early to head to his mother's, but he had
no place else to go right now. As he walked past the ice
cream parlor, he spied a young family seated on one of the
benches out front. A little girl, maybe three or four years old,
licked at her rapidly melting cone while the mother and father
talked and laughed over her head. The man and woman
seemed so in sync, like he and Becky had been.

Oliver's boyfriend, Todd, cycled past on a surrey,
another reminder of what he'd lost by breaking things off
with her. Just hanging out and having fun, which he'd thought
would be enough. He was a fool. A pussy who had been
afraid to make an actual commitment. Now? Now he was a
guy who couldn't get the woman having his baby to spare
him a minute to talk.

His mother was checking on her pot roast when Nate let
himself into her house.

"Hey, Mom."

She straightened, her eyes wide. "Nate, honey! You're

early."

"Yeah, well." He placed the bakery box on the back counter. "I stopped by Sweet Escape."

"Ooh, that place has the best goodies!" She opened the box and peered inside. "Oh, dear. No strawberry shorties."

"I think Becky ate the last one."

"You saw Becky?"

He nodded.

"How did that go?"

"What do you mean?"

She clicked her tongue. "Nate, you're my son. I know you almost as well as I know myself. You miss her."

"I do."

"Then talk to her."

"I tried. She doesn't want to talk to me."

"What happened between you two?"

It was on the tip of his tongue to say she was the reason they weren't together, but that wasn't fair. Suddenly she gasped.

"Oh, honey! I know I begged you to move back in here with me. I'm the reason you're not together?"

"That's not it, Mom. Yeah, that had something to do

with it but it was my stupid idea to end things. And now…"
He shut up quick.

"And now what, Nate?"

"Nothing." He wasn't ready to talk more about the
baby. It was too new. Too painful that she was now keeping
him at arms' length because he hadn't the balls to take a risk
and try to make something real when he'd had the chance.

The doorbell rang and his mother dropped the subject to
hurry to the front door. Dave McCall soon stood in the foyer
and, now that Nate studied him, he could see the physical
similarities between them. They were both tall and broad and,
though he had his mother's blue eyes, their faces were of a
similar shape.

"Hello, Nate."

Nate nodded. "Mr. McCall."

"Please. Call me Dave?"

At least he hadn't asked him to call him Dad. "Dave."

"Come in, Dave." His mother hooked her arm through
his and led him through the living area. "You're early."

Dave glanced at Nate, his brows drawn together. "I was
hoping to talk to you."

"Me?"

The guy smirked, but there was warmth in his eyes. "Don't you think it's about time?"

His mother bit her lip and nodded. Nate did likewise and they settled on the couches. His mother sat close to Dave and Nate sat opposite.

"I know your mom told you a little about what happened back then."

"When you left us, you mean?"

"Nate." His mother's voice was soft.

Dave held up a hand. "No, Donna. He's right. I left you both. It was not an easy decision to make, but I made it. I left."

Nate raised his brows. The guy had the balls to take responsibility. That counted for something.

"She also said you came back," Nate said. "I don't remember."

"You were a little guy. Younger than those kids you're coaching."

"You know about that?"

"I have a lot of time to make up for, don't I? I've been asking around."

"I bet you've heard an earful," Nate said.

266

"Yes, there doesn't seem to be any shortage of information to be had in Cypress Corners. Don't worry about my carrying any tales," Dave went on. "I haven't told Ashlyn that you're her brother yet."

"I know."

"You do?"

Nate nodded. "I went to see her today, just to say hello."

"You did?" his mother asked.

"Did you tell her?" Dave asked.

"It's not my place."

"You're a good man, Nate. From all accounts, you've already made friends here. People respect you."

"I guess."

"It's true." Dave covered his mother's hand with one of his. "Your mother did a wonderful job. I can never get the time back that I lost. It's my greatest regret."

Nate's throat tightened. "I missed having a dad."

"We used to toss the ball around, you know. When I was back for a while before Ashlyn was born."

"My mom said she was sick?"

"She was, yes. With a type of anemia. Steroids and transfusions… It was a lot for a little girl to take."

"I'm sorry."

"She's a strong kid." Pride was clear in his voice. "Like her brother, I think."

Nate stared at this man he didn't know, and felt a stirring in his chest. There was a connection here. He could feel it. He might be in the middle of a mess with Becky, but he could do something about this particular entanglement.

He stood. "How about a beer, Dave?"

His father grinned. "Sounds good."

***

On Monday morning, Becky moved around the condo quietly. It was silly, thinking that Nate could hear her from across the hall. She knew how well this place was built. Still, just knowing he was over there getting himself ready for work was enough to set her pulse racing.

"Hormones," she chided herself.

As she buttoned her camp shirt, she noticed that her breasts filled out the fabric more than they had before. That seemed like a nice tradeoff for nausea every morning.

"Ready for work, Lovebug?" she asked her belly.

She laughed to herself. It seemed like a fitting nickname, since she'd met Nate during the tale end of the spring season for the pesky insects. It was kind of sweet and endearing, and she chose to ignore the fact that every spring and fall she had to wipe hundreds of the things off the front of her car before they ruined the paint job. Lovebugs were another reason she preferred to ride her bike around Cypress, at least until her own little lovebug came to be.

She'd hidden out at Joy and Zach's place yesterday, out by the far lakeshore. No going to the Chapman barbecue or hanging around the town square for her, thanks. She was in no mood to run into Nate again.

She drained her cup of herbal tea, and then set the mug in the sink. Mondays were always busy at the Institute and today shouldn't be any different. Dr. Robbins was due to head up to Tallahassee for a conference on Wednesday, so she knew he would have lots of notes for her regarding the running of the place in his absence.

There was no sign of Nate as she made her way down to her garage. She saw his big truck, so she'd beat him downstairs this morning. She'd made a game of it, seeing if he was still here when she would leave for work. It was childish, but it managed to keep her from pining after the big idiot.

The morning was bright, and the usual summer weather pattern had moved in. Heat all day, followed by popup thunderstorms in the afternoon. She'd long grown accustomed to the quirky Florida weather, though. In fact, she'd come to look forward to the slight change of seasons they saw in Central Florida particularly. The leaves even changed color, but usually not until December.

"Happy Monday!" Harmony called as Becky arrived at the reception desk.

"Back atcha," Becky said. "How was your weekend?"

"Another Sunday, another barbecue." Harmony put her hands on her hips. "We missed you, you know."

"I hung out with my sister out at the far lakeshore."

"The love shack," Harmony joked. "I have very fond memories of that place."

Becky chuckled. It was true that several Cypress romances had begun in that little tent-cabin over the past few years.

"They're building a house out by the stables, though," she told Harmony. "That means the shack will be available again soon."

Harmony winked. "It doubt it'll be vacant for long. See

270

you later."

"Later."

Harmony went down to her office as Becky clicked through the programs to pull up the day's appointments. Nate's name popped up, causing those silly flutters. She really should get over him, but she now knew she'd not only been half in love with him back then. She'd been all the way, head over heels in love with him even as a teenager. Now that she was carrying their little lovebug, that love had set up permanent residence in her heart.

"And he can never know about it," she said to herself.

"Know about what?" Nate asked.

Her traitorous heart skipped as she looked up at him. "Nate," she breathed. So much for avoiding him.

"Good morning, Becks." He held up a familiar bright green bakery bag. "I brought you some strawberry shorties."

Her stomach growled loudly and she flushed. "You didn't have to do that."

"I know you like them." He shrugged and folded his arms. "Besides, consider them a bribe."

"A bribe?"

"I need to ask you a favor."

Oh, those lines creasing his brow couldn't mean good news. She'd seen them before, the night he needed to talk. Still, she couldn't refuse him anything, not that she'd share that little nugget of truth with him.

"With these in my hot little hands, Bugs?" Closing her eyes, she opened the bag and breathed in. "Mmm. Ask me anything."

"There's been a lot going on right now, and I'd really like to talk to a friend."

Ick, that word. She looked at him again. "Friend?"

"Aren't we still friends, Becks?"

And that was all they were. Period. End of sentence.

"Yes, we are."

"Then can I come over tonight?"

Her heart jumped. "Tonight?"

He held up his hands.

"I promise to keep my hands to myself." He gave her a crooked smile, looking like the kid he'd been when she'd first fallen for him. "Cross my heart."

Did he have to be so charming and adorable?

She couldn't avoid him, but she was a woman who knew what she wanted and didn't want. It was just her too bad that they were the same thing.

"Okay."

His relief was a living thing as his brow smoothed and those lines around his sculpted lips disappeared. Just what was going on with him?

"Thanks, Becks. I'll bring pizza."

She arched brow, going for cool detachment at this minute. "First shorties and now pizza? You sure know…" She stopped herself. "My weaknesses."

His expression cleared. "Not even close."

He turned down the hallway and disappeared into his office. She nibbled on a shortie, grateful that she'd stopped herself from finishing her thought out loud. He knew the way to her heart. He should, shouldn't he?

He'd lived there for ten years now.

Chapter 22

"I'm glad you're happy, Mom." Nate took a long pull of his beer and waited a beat for her to absorb that disclosure. "But I'm not coming to another family dinner."

He could feel his mother's disappointment through the phone. "Nate, you have to get to know your sister."

"I will. It's just a lot to take in all at once."

"Ashlyn is just lovely," she said. "I've thought that from the first time I met her."

"Yeah, she seems like a good kid."

"And she would undoubtedly like to know her brother."

"Half-brother," he said in reflex. "Does she know?"

"No, your father hasn't told her yet."

He recalled the irritation on the girl's face when he'd walked into the bakery the other day. She was Team Becky, and he suspected that only one reason was her relationship with Tom Rollins. During his time in Cypress Corners he'd seen that Becks really was the center of the community family.

"Mom, Ashlyn is not exactly my biggest fan right now."

"Why not?" She harrumphed. "You're a wonderful guy."

Nate rolled his eyes. "Thanks, but she's seeing Becky's brother and Tom isn't too happy with me right now."

"Because of your silly breakup with Becky?"

"That's not the only reason."

She grew quiet again, and he could imagine the wheels turning in her head. "Nate, what did you do?"

He couldn't tell her about how Becky didn't want him around her or their baby. Not again. It was all so raw, and he and Becky weren't in a place where he'd feel comfortable giving away her secrets. She already wanted his head on a spike. He wouldn't hand her his balls, too.

"Nothing. It'll be okay."

"Are you sure, honey? Do you want to talk?"

"Talk?" Since when did she want to talk about anything other than her most recent infatuation or heartbreak? That thought made him feel a little disloyal and a whole lot crappy, so he fell back into dutiful son mode again. "No, thanks."

"You know where I live," she quipped.

He drained his beer and set the bottle down. "I do."

"Have a good night, honey."

"You too, Mom."

He disconnected the call and set his phone on the

counter. When had his life turned into such a mess? If he was being completely honest with himself, he would admit that he'd been coasting along before coming to Cypress. He'd had his job with the county, which had been boring but productive work. He'd had a rental house he shared with his mother, for God's sake. He'd had no kind of romantic life to speak of, let alone a love life. He couldn't even remember the last time he'd gotten laid before reconnecting with Becky. Now?

Now he had job he honestly loved. He'd settled his mother in a home of her own. But he also had a father he didn't really know and a sister who didn't like him very much. And to top it all off, the woman who was having his baby wanted nothing to do with him.

He couldn't believe that with all the people recently added to his life he felt completely alone. He'd made connections at the Institute and the Sales Center. Sure he was friends with Zach, but he couldn't talk to the guy who was with Becky's sister. The doorbell rang, saving him from further wallowing.

It was a delivery guy with the pizza he'd ordered. He paid the kid and shut his own door. He'd told Becky he'd bring pizza tonight, and the least he could do was keep that promise. He knocked on her door, shifting from foot to foot. She opened it, and he was completely gut-punched.

Her skin was flushed and her hair a wild red cloud around her. She wore some kind of slouchy pajama pants with flamingos all over them and a bright pink tank top to match. He could see a hint of the lacy bra she wore underneath and he felt a flash of want. She looked sweet and hot, two things he'd never thought could happen at once before he'd gotten back together with her.

"Dinner, Becks."

She brushed some strands of hair behind one ear and stepped back. "Then you may enter."

He flashed a small smile. "Thanks."

He stepped in and crossed to the kitchen, and then placed the pizza box on the counter. "I was going to bring beer, but I didn't want to drink alone."

His gaze drifted to her midsection, and she splayed one hand on her belly.

"No drinks for the lovebug," she said.

"Lovebug?"

Her flush grew deeper. "That's what I've been calling it."

He chuckled. "Plecia nearctica. That's a pretty name for a girl."

She laughed, her eyes bright. "Um, no."

It hung between them, their child and the connection they already had. She might deny it, but he knew he'd never felt for another woman what he did for Becky.

"Let's eat," he said.

They began to share their meal, seated at the tall counter.

She poured them each a glass of sparkling water. "Are you sure you don't want a beer? I still have a couple of yours in the fridge."

"No. I had one before coming over and it didn't do much to improve things."

Leaning an elbow on the counter, she turned in her stool to face him. "Nate, what's going on?"

"Ah, Becks. I don't even know where to start."

"It's always been my experience that the best place to start is at the beginning."

"That's logical." He smiled. "I thought I was the scientific thinker."

"The word you're searching for is geek."

"True that." He took a breath. "I met my father."

***

Becky stared at him for a beat. His disclosure certainly explained those frown lines.

"Oh, Bugs."

His eyes were shiny and he rubbed a hand over his face. "I never expected this." A small smile curved his lips. "I used to ask my mother all the time when I was young. Pestered her, actually."

She couldn't help herself, and reached out to touch his rigid forearm. He seemed to relax a bit.

"When did you find out?" she asked softly.

"About a week ago."

She blinked. "That's why you moved back, isn't it? To the condo?"

"Yes." His gaze ran over her. "That's not the only reason, though."

When her cheeks grew hot, she inwardly cursed her fair coloring. "Your father, Nate." She squared her shoulders. "Did you know him?"

"No. Not even a little bit," he said. "He and my mom got back together when I was a kid, but I don't remember."

"Back together? What happened, then?"

He shrugged. "I guess they were together for a little while and then my sister got sick."

"Your what?"

He gave a short laugh. "Yeah, that was my first reaction too."

"Was she okay? Your sister?"

"Half-sister, actually. She was sick for a while, I guess."

"That sucks, Nate. For all of you."

He raked a hand through his hair. "She's here in Cypress, too. You know her."

"I know her? Who is she?"

"Ashlyn."

That stunned her. "Ashlyn? Ashlyn McCall?"

"Yep."

"Ashlyn, the girl who's dating my brother?"

"Yep," he said again. "And she can't stand me."

"I don't think that's true."

He leveled a look at her. "Your brother would probably like to pin me to a board."

She shook her head. "What?"

"Like a bug, Becks."

"Oh." She chuckled. "Yeah, he would probably like that."

"How did everything get so fucked up?"

"I can only speak for what used to be us, Bugs."

"Yeah, used to be. I fucked that up too."

She wasn't going to let him off the hook, or the board for that matter. "You made a unilateral decision, Nate. You didn't take my feelings into consideration."

"And you wouldn't get back together with me."

"When you demanded it? No."

His nostrils flared. "I have a father I don't know, a sister who hates me and a girlfriend who doesn't want to be with me."

"Girlfriend?" Her heart stuttered. "Since when?"

He touched her face, his fingers gentle on her cheek. "You're my Becks." His gaze dipped to her belly again before meeting hers. "You're having our baby."

"That's not news," she whispered.

He brought his brow to hers. "And it isn't news that I never stopped wanting you."

He kissed her, first a feathery touch and then with more delicious pressure. She knew she should end this, but his kiss was spiced and hot and just what she'd been craving. Their tongues met, and she just closed her eyes and savored this familiar heat between them.

"Oh, Bugs." She let her head fall back as he kissed her throat.

"God, Becks." He licked and nipped at her skin. "I want you."

She wanted him, too. So badly she was nearly shaking. "Nate."

He came up to cup her face in his hands. "Please, Becks."

Maybe it was the hormones. Maybe it was the pizza. Maybe it was the fact that she'd always loved him, darn him anyway.

"Take me to bed," she whispered.

He swept her up into his arms and they made their roundabout way to her bedroom. His hands were quick, his touch magical, as her body responded more sharply than ever before.

When he lowered her to the bed, when he closed his mouth over one nipple, she cried out. She felt everything so sharply, wanted him so fiercely, that she reached down for him and guided him inside of her.

"Becks, wait." His breathing was harsh and his expression intense.

"W-Why?" She didn't stop touching him, tracing every perfect muscle with eager hands. "Why wait?"

"I don't have a condom."

That startled a laugh out of her. "I think the horse has left the barn."

He barked out a strangled laugh, and then proceeded to fill her completely. His every move was perfect, and it took very little for her to soar toward climax. As he moved, fast and sure, she reached her peak. He didn't stop, his body hot and hard as he drew every bit of passion out of her.

As she neared another orgasm, he began to shake.

"Becks!"

He came inside her, holding her tightly in his arms as he gave himself over to his release. She gasped for air as the sensation of bliss seemed to ooze from every cell in her body.

"Becks." His voice was soft, rasping, as he kissed the side of her neck. "Mmm."

Her eyes were still closed, her body still tingling, as she ran one hand through his hair. "I love you, Nate."

He froze against her, and she realized what she'd just said. In the next second he sat up, jostling her.

"Listen, Becks."

Any afterglow of bliss left her in a rush that took her breath. Opening her eyes, she watched him. "What?"

"I…" His eyes darted around the room and she wished in that moment that she had the power to turn back the clock. Just a few seconds was all she would need.

"Nate, I didn't mean to say that."

His expression in his eyes was flat and his lips thinned. It was clear that he didn't believe her.

"It doesn't matter."

She gaped at him. "What doesn't matter, exactly?"

He stood beside the bed and put on his clothes with quick, jerking motions. "What you said."

"What I said," she repeated. "I can't believe you." Anger surged, mingled with acute sadness. "No, I can. You say that you don't know your father. That your sister doesn't like you?"

"Becks."

"That's all your fault, Nate." She held the rumpled sheets over herself, clutching them tightly in an effort to keep him from seeing just how hurt she was by his dismissal. "All of it."

"Why?"

"Because you keep everyone from getting too close."

He waved a hand. "I didn't come here for this."

"For what, exactly? For a sympathy lay?"

He appeared stunned by her vulgarity, but it felt good to say it.

He clenched his teeth, a muscle visibly ticking in his jaw, and growled softly. "I meant, I didn't come here with the goal of ending up in your bed."

"Yeah well, you did. More fool me."

He stood there, his big feet braced apart and his T-shirt creased and crooked. "Becks."

"Get out."

He let out a string of curses she'd never heard him utter before. "Fine."

Then he left. She held her breath until she heard her door slam shut. Then she cried for herself. For him, darn him. And for their baby.

"You matter, Lovebug," she whispered. "You will never doubt that."

It would be a cold day in Cypress Corners before she ever let him into her bed again, let alone into her heart.

Chapter 23

Nate's phone was ringing. Or his alarm was chiming. From inside his skull. When he'd left Becky's last night, he'd been confused and more than a little pissed. Finishing off the beers in his fridge had been a terrible idea. It hadn't made any difference in the end. Even buzzed, he'd had trouble falling asleep.

Stretching over toward the nightstand, he grabbed his phone and tapped it about a hundred times before the damn thing stopped dinging. Rolling onto his back, he flung an arm over his gritty eyes and groaned. His stomach clenched and his mouth was bone dry.

By the time he got into the shower, and let the hot water pulsate on him, he began to feel a little bit better. With the pounding in his head subdued, he couldn't keep last night's events from flashing behind his aching eyelids, though.

He'd gone over to talk to Becky. His best friend. His…he wasn't even sure who she was to him but he'd known he needed her. They'd talked, and laughed a little, which had made him feel so much better. Then he'd had her again, and it had been hotter than he'd been imagining over these past weeks. She'd nearly turned him inside out. After, when he could think again, he'd heard her say something to him no woman ever had.

She loved him? When the hell had that happened?

He swallowed a couple of ibuprofen and got dressed for work. There would be no avoiding her today, but he would try his damnedest to give her space. A lot of space.

Somehow he'd managed to make things worse. Maybe she was right. Maybe this *was* all his fault. His family crap. His lack of any real relationships. He'd never given his all for something real. He'd never even tried.

Now? With reality staring him straight in the face? He'd screwed up big time. Picking up his phone again, he tapped on his mother's name.

"Nate?" Her voice sounded wary. "What's wrong?"

Everything. It seemed to be a recurring theme for him.

"Nothing, Mom. I need you to do me a favor."

"Anything, honey."

"Can we have a family dinner at your place tonight? A real family dinner."

"Real?

"Yes. I want to have a meal with my father and half… With my father and sister."

She sobbed audibly. "Nate, that would be lovely."

"Lovely or not, I have a lot to make up for."

"What are you talking about?"

He couldn't think of an answer at that second, his head still throbbing dully and his throat tight. "Just let me know what time, and what you'd like me to bring."

"Just bring yourself, honey." There was a long pause over the line. "And Becky?"

"That's not going to happen, Mom."

"That's a shame."

"I know." *Shame on me.* "I hope I can fix that too, but it's a whole other situation."

"I'll make sure your father and sister are here tonight, then. And Nate?"

"Yeah?"

"I love you."

Those words again, but he'd heard them from his mother a million times. Funny how different they felt when they came from the woman he loved.

His heart thudded. He loved Becky? He loved her!

"Nate?"

"What? Love you too, Mom."

He disconnected the call and slumped down onto his couch. He loved Becky. His Becks. Why the hell hadn't he figured that out before now?

She wouldn't believe him if he told her now. No. He'd made such a mess of everything, first breaking things off and then insisting they get back together because she got pregnant.

"Real dick move," he told himself.

First things first. He had to get through his workday without getting too close to Becky. He had to figure his crap out before he went to her with his heart in his hand.

Around three that afternoon, someone knocked on the open door to his office. Nate looked up to find the director standing there, an expectant look on his face.

"Dr. Robbins, come in."

The man nodded and came closer. "Nate, I've never been one to give any credence to the flotsam and jetsam floating around Cypress Corners."

Nate nodded. "You know."

"Know?" He closed the door and settled his wiry frame in the chair opposite. "What, exactly, do you believe I know?"

"About Becky and me."

"I knew you two were dating." His eyes narrowed behind his glasses. "She's my best girl, you know. My right hand."

"I know that, sir."

"She doesn't have a father to take up her cause, and I'm more than willing to fill that role."

"She's lucky to have you."

"I'm the lucky one, from the first day she bounced in here insisting she was the perfect person to help whip the Institute into shape." He smiled. "I admit I'm not the best at organization."

Nate's lips twitched. "You get the job done."

"Thank you for that. Now, about Becky."

Nate folded his hands and leaned toward the director. "Doc, I know I screwed up. In more ways than one. I promise you, I'm going to make things right."

"That's good to hear, but there's more at stake than hearts here."

Nate nodded. "The baby."

Dr. Robbins gasped. "There's a baby?"

"I thought you knew." He spread his hands wide.

"Please don't say anything to Becky?"

"I would never." He crossed his arms and frowned. "You're going to make things right, you said?"

"I am."

The man gave a sharp nod. "Good." He stood. "I don't want to see her crying again."

"She was crying?"

"Softly, yes. This morning at her desk. Nearly broke my heart."

As if Nate didn't feel low enough, that did it. "I am more sorry than I can say."

The director's brows snapped together. "You better say, and soon. Our girl needs you."

With those words, Dr. Robbins left his office. Nate would fix things. He would have to take a leap into the unknown, something he was never any good at doing.

"Man up, Bauer," he said to himself.

When he arrived at his mother's house, he saw two cars parked in her driveway. One was a Tesla that had to belong to Dave, and another was a little blue Mini. He guessed that was his sister's, and thought it suited her. Small but mighty.

He could still remember the determination on her face

that afternoon in the bakery. She didn't take anything from anybody, let alone the big brother she didn't know.

His mother met him at the door with a hug and an encouraging squeeze to one shoulder. "Dinner first, Nate?"

"No, if that's all right." He stepped into the house and found Dave and Ashlyn sitting in the living room. Both looked at him expectantly, his father with arched brows and his sister with a slight frown.

"Hi," he said.

His father stood and shook Nate's hand. "Hi, there."

"Nate." Ashlyn crossed her arms. "I hear you're my brother."

Blowing out a breath, he crossed to her. "Ashlyn, I want to say I'm sorry."

Her brows rose now. "You didn't do anything to me."

"I didn't make an effort when I found out, either." He scoffed. "Seems I never do, but I'm going to now."

She tilted her head to one side. "What are you saying, Nate?"

"I'm saying that you're my sister and I want us to have a real relationship."

"Real?"

"Yeah. Seems I've always had a problem with real. Will you give me a chance?"

Her bottom lip quivered, but she met his gaze evenly. "I will."

Something bloomed in his chest and he placed a hand on her shoulder. "Thank you." He turned to his father. "Dave, I want the same with you. If you want it."

Dave wrapped him in a bear hug, startling the air out of him. "Son, I've always wanted this." He leaned back. "I've always wanted you."

Whoa. He hadn't expected his father's words to have such a profound effect, but his world seemed to tilt. "Thanks, Dave."

They shared a smile and his mother let out a sigh of contentment.

"Oh, honey. You've taken care of me all of these years," she said. "At the cost of your own relationships."

"I don't blame you for my mistakes, Mom."

"Is this about your girlfriend?" Dave asked.

"How did you know?" Nate held up a hand. "Never mind. Ashlyn is dating Becky's little brother."

"Tom isn't a fan of yours right now," Ashlyn said. "And

you know why."

"I do."

"Why?" his mother asked. "Is this about the baby?"

"I swear I'll tell you everything, Mom. Soon, I promise." He looked back at Ashlyn. "I'm going to try to fix things with Becky, but that's a whole other mess I've made."

Ashlyn bit her lip, her face scrunched as if in thought, and then touched his arm. "I know where you can find her tonight."

"You do?"

She grinned a very familiar smile and nodded.

***

At the End Zone, Becky sat with Joy and Caro. It was just the three of them, which she suspected was due to the fact that she had no guy in her own life so they'd left theirs to fend for themselves tonight.

"The place is pretty busy for a Tuesday night." Caro lifted her mojito and took a sip. "Mmm. I bet I can make a dessert that tastes like this."

"If anyone can, you can," Becky said.

"Ooh, how about a margarita munchie?" Joy put in.

Caro chuckled. "How about you leave the naming to

Ashlyn."

Becky twisted the plastic stirrer from her tequila sunrise, all juice no tequila, and nodded. "What do you know about Ashlyn, Caro?"

"Know?" She licked her lips and shrugged. "I know she's a good kid. Sweet. A hard worker."

"What about her family?" Becky pressed.

"Her dad just moved to Cypress Corners," Caro said.

"Tom said he's a nice man," Joy said. "Why are you asking?"

"She's Nate's sister."

Both of the other women wore matching expressions of surprise.

"You're kidding, right?" Joy asked first.

Becky shook her head. "Nope. Mr. McCall is Nate's father. I'm surprised you hadn't heard about it."

"I just bet Lettie knows," Caro said. "She seems to know what cards to show and which ones to keep under her bonnet."

"Or something like that," Joy said.

"It's just a lot, you know?" Becky asked. "He's had a few surprises over the past couple of weeks."

"Are you making excuses, Becky?" Joy snorted. "I've never known you to do that before."

"She's never been in love before," Caro said.

Becky started, and then gave a small nod. "Yeah, and it sucks."

"It doesn't have to," Caro said.

Becky took another sip of her juice. "Easy for you to say. Both of you. You have your guys. My guy doesn't want anything real."

"He's having a baby with you," Joy said, her voice low. "It doesn't get any more real than that."

"But he doesn't love me."

Caro clicked her tongue. "Are you sure?"

Becky sniffed, refusing to start crying again. "I am. He's never told me so, not even when he was insisting we be together."

"He insisted?" Caro asked. "That's pretty real, too."

"After he broke up with me, Caro. Only when he heard about the baby."

"What a tool," Joy said. "Want me to kick his ass?"

Becky managed a smile. "No. My mess, my solution."

"*You're* going to kick his ass?" Caro asked.

"No. I just…" Becky stopped as an oh-so-familiar song began to play from the digital jukebox. "Oh, no," she groaned.

"What's wrong?" Joy asked. "Nausea?"

"No. It's that friggin' song."

"What's the song got to…?" Caro began. "Oh."

"Sis, we don't have to stay here."

Becky braced her hands on the table. "No. I'm not leaving." She stood. "I am going to shut that darn song off, though."

She turned toward the jukebox and froze. There was no question who had played that song. It was Nate, and he was standing there beside it. He wore jeans and a plaid shirt, and an expression of hope clear on his face.

"Bugs," she whispered.

"Is it too late, Becks?" he asked. "To apologize?"

The song again. That darn song. She couldn't seem to make her feet move. "I can't do this."

He walked closer to her. "Becks, I was wrong."

She blinked. "Okay, I'm listening."

"I was wrong to break up with you." He took her hand in his, and his touch was warm and sure. "I was even more wrong to try to get back together for the sake of the lovebug."

"Lovebug," Caro said behind her.

"Aw," Joy chimed in.

"You were wrong?" Becky asked.

He nodded, caressing the back of her hand with his thumb. "About everything, Becks. I love you."

She was stunned. Her heart froze, and then sped up until it raced. "Y-you love me?"

He smiled, his eyes bright. "I think I've always loved you."

"You love me," she repeated.

"I do." He touched her cheek in that way she loved. "Do you still love me?"

Tears stung her eyes and she began to sob. "Yes."

He held her close, rocking her a little as she cried all over his shirt. His big hands rubbed her back and she didn't care if they were making a spectacle there in the middle of the End Zone.

"Marry me?" he said, his mouth close to her ear.

She sucked in a breath and leaned away from him, studying his beloved face. "Marry you?" Oh, she had to know what this was about. "Why?"

"Because I love you, Becks." He shook his head. "Not because of the baby. Not because of this thing we've always had between us. Because I love you." He kissed her, quick and sweet, and pulled back. "And you love me."

"I do," she said, echoing his earlier words.

He arched a brow, a crooked smile on his face. "So?"

Her heart seemed to swell and she nearly floated up onto her toes to kiss him. "Yes, I'll marry you."

He kissed her fully then, and as the song faded into the next selection she heard everyone in the place cheering for them.

Epilogue

Nate held Becky close to him under the quilt, burying his nose in her hair as he breathed in her sweet hot scent. He could hear the crickets, their songs loud and long outside the screened window of the tent-cabin. Southern Field, and Wood, crickets making trilling to signal the coming end of Florida summer along with the buzzing of Cicadas. September was the most musical of all the seasons.

"Hear that?" he rasped, nibbling on her earlobe.

She sighed and cuddled closer. "Can't help it, Bugs."

"Thank your sister for me."

She laughed. "Like the love shack, do you?"

"It's the perfect getaway, close to home."

"Home?" She brushed a hair off his brow. "You're home, Nate?"

"Anywhere you are."

"You have a romantic streak I never imagined."

"Back in school, when I was an idiot? Or when I screwed things up here?"

"You were smart enough to make me fall in love with you."

He felt that warmth in his chest again. "Yeah, I did."

"Speaking of home, what are we going to do about our living situation?"

"Mrs. Barnes called me when she heard our news." He shook his head. "She has a direct line to Lettie."

"And?"

"She's going to sublet to Derek Stone's sister. Abby, I think?"

"Oh, Abby! She'll be a nice neighbor."

"We'll have to look for a bigger place when the baby comes, you know."

She narrowed her eyes. "What have you done?"

"Nothing yet. But Eli has a few places he wants to show us."

"I'll just bet. No grass grows under his feet, or something like that."

"I'll keep you posted, Becks."

"You better. This will be our forever home for the lovebug."

He marveled at that for a long minute. "So what did your mom have to say?"

"Lots, as usual." She laughed. "She's thrown herself into the wedding plans." She turned and propped herself on her elbow. "She wants to have it at the inn, around Thanksgiving. Your sister will be in the wedding, and she's going to help with the flowers. I'll get with Caro about the cake."

"Whatever you want, Becks."

"Leaving it to me, Bugs?"

He kissed her. "Always."

"As it should be," she teased.

He lowered his head to her belly. "Hear that, Lovebug? Your mommy sounds happy."

"I am." She settled back down, a sweetly smug expression on her beautiful face. "Are you?"

"Couldn't be happier."

He closed his eyes and let out a breath of intense satisfaction. He had his Becks in his life. For good. He had his family and friends there in Cypress Corners. More importantly, he had the life he'd always wanted. It was real. And more than he could have imagined when he'd walked into the Institute that spring morning. He couldn't ignore her, or the connection between them that had only grown stronger.

He'd be happy to let his Becks bug him until the end of time.

About the Author

JoMarie DeGioia is a bestselling author of Historical and Contemporary Romance. She's known Mickey Mouse from the "inside," has been a copyeditor for her tiny town's newspaper, and a bookseller. She is the author of over 40 Romances, and writes Young Adult Fantasy/Adventure stories and Paranormal Romance too. She gets lost in DIY projects around the house and works out plot ideas during long runs. She divides her time between Central Florida and New England.

Discover other books by JoMarie DeGioia

The Bridgewater Brides series, including

The Heir's Treasure

The Viscount's Vixen

The Earl's Beauty

The Gentlemen Undercover series, including

A Hero and a Gentleman

The Shopgirls of Bond Street series, including

That Determined Mister Latham

The Dashing Nobles series, including

More Than Passion

Pride and Fire

Just Perfect

More Than Charming

The Cypress Corners series, including

Finding Harmony

Taming Jake

Loving Cassie

Winning Ben

Showing Jessie

Seeing Shannon (Barefoot Bay World novella)

Dreaming Eli

Giving Chase (Barefoot Bay World novella)

Kissing Bree

Wishing Joy

Bugging Nate

The Gifted YA Fantasy/Adventure Trilogy, including

Gifted

Braunachs of the Dell series, including

Luke's Gold

Patrick's Promise

Connect with me online

Twitter: https://twitter.com/JoMarieDeGioia

Facebook:

https://www.facebook.com/JoMarie.DeGioia.Author

Website: www.jomariedegioia.com

www.ingramcontent.com/pod-product-compliance
Lightning Source LLC
Chambersburg PA
CBHW070000200626
46811CB00021B/2490